P9-BZT-001

Praise for

Elliot and the Goblin War

"Never before have the secrets of the Underworld been exposed with such flair and self-assured hilarity. It is a winning combination, one that is sure to delight young readers eager to dip their toe into the world of the fantastical. A perfect mix of goblin antics, a likeable hero, and droll humor! Even the most reluctant of readers will be pulled in."

—R. L. LaFevers, author of *Theodosia and the Eyes of Horus*

"Jen Nielsen invites us into a frightful, funny world where the good guys work hard, the bad guys poof (unless you order them not to), chocolate is a weapon, and pickles are bait. I want to live there. Crown this book King of Goblin comedy and fright. I'm an Elliot fan for life—and that's in Brownie years."

—Ruth McNally Barshaw, creator of Ellie McDoodle

Elliot
and the
Goblin War

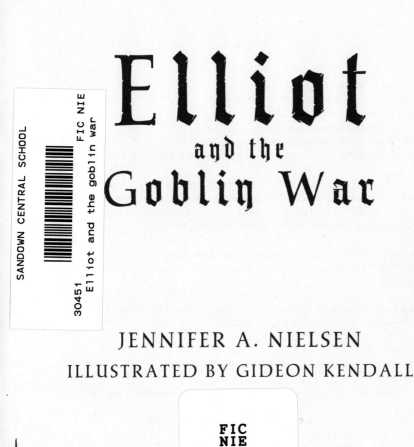

Elliot
and the
Goblin War

JENNIFER A. NIELSEN

ILLUSTRATED BY GIDEON KENDALL

FIC
NIE

sourcebooks
jabberwocky

11.09

4/12 Follett

Published by Sourcebooks Jabberwocky, an imprint of Sourcebooks, Inc.
P.O. Box 4410, Naperville, Illinois 60567-4410
(630) 961-3900
Fax: (630) 961-2168
www.jabberwockykids.com

Library of Congress Cataloging-in-Publication data is on file with the publisher.

Source of Production: Sheridan Books, Chelsea, Michigan, USA
Date of Production: March 2011
Run Number: 14727

Printed and bound in the United States of America.
SB 10 9 8 7 6 5 4 3 2

For Bridger, who can become anything he wants.

Contents

Warning!

As of today, there are only seven children who have ever read this book and lived to tell about it. Ninety-five children successfully read the first chapter, but upon beginning chapter 2, they started blabbering in some language known only as "Flibberish," which makes it very hard to tell their parents why they can't finish their homework. Thirty-eight children made it halfway through this wretched book before their brains simply shut down and they began sucking their thumbs through their noses.

But these are minor problems compared to what happened to those who read the final chapters of this book. The only thing known for sure is that something in chapter 15 seems to make body parts fall off.

If you're very brave, one of those who would battle a dragon with only a toothpick for a sword, perhaps you are willing to take your chances and turn the page. But before you read even one more sentence, be sure that you have told your family who gets your favorite toys if you do not survive this book. Read it now, if you dare. But don't say you haven't been warned, for this is the story that unfolds the mysteries of the Underworld. Turn the page and begin *Elliot and the Goblin War*.

Where Elliot Gets a Little Scared

WHEN HE WAS EIGHT YEARS OLD, ELLIOT PENSTER STARTED an interspecies war. Don't blame him. As anyone who has ever started an interspecies war will tell you, it's not that difficult to do.

Elliot had spent the evening trick-or-treating. Everyone thought he was dressed as a hobo, but he wasn't. He didn't have money for a Halloween costume, and so he'd just gone in his everyday clothes.

On that night, his everyday clothes were a pair of his big brother's old jeans with a hole in one knee, a T-shirt that sort of fit if he didn't lift his arms up, and a long-sleeved plaid shirt over it that *did* fit. He also wore two different shoes, which weren't part of his everyday clothes. It's just that he couldn't find their matches.

Either way, he was on his way home with a big sack of candy, which is all that ever really matters on Halloween. He dipped his face into his sack and sniffed up the blend of chocolate, fruit, and sugar smells. And lead? Elliot pulled an orange pencil from his sack and then dropped it back in. Who gives pencils for Halloween? Probably the dentist over on Apple Lane.

Elliot wrapped his sack up tight to keep the smell inside until he got home. He planned to share a few candies with his family and then go wild with the rest in one night of sugar-crazed insanity.

"Help!" a voice cried.

Elliot turned to see a little girl running toward him, dressed as an Elf. Her right arm flailed wildly, and in her left arm she carried a sack almost as big as she was. Every time she screamed, all the dogs in the area howled. Chasing her were two kids about his own size dressed as Goblins.

"Hey!" Elliot yelled at them. "You're not supposed to take someone else's candy!"

Elliot ran toward the kids in the Goblin suits. He tossed his heavy sack of candy over his shoulder then swung it toward them. It hit one Goblin in the shoulder and knocked him into the other. They fell on top of each other on the ground.

"Stay out of this," the Goblin on the bottom snarled. "You're only a human boy."

"Don't make fun of my costume!" Elliot yelled. "Just because you can afford a cool costume doesn't make you cool."

The Goblin on the top rolled to his feet. "We don't want to be cool. We want to be scary."

"My sister cooks dinners that are scarier than you," Elliot said. It wasn't an insult to his sister. She really did.

"You want to see scary?" the Goblin asked. He crouched down on all fours and let out a growling sound that Elliot didn't think any human voice could make.

Then something happened, something Elliot had never seen a costume be able to do before. Not even the expensive ones. It began bubbling, as if it had become a vat of black, boiling oil. Ripples of bubbles started small but gradually grew bigger, almost as if the Goblin itself were growing in size.

Elliot's eyes widened. He'd seen things like this in the movies before. Even if this was only a costume, it was still a lot scarier in person than watching it in a theater with a bucket of popcorn on his lap. He didn't want to watch it, and yet he found it impossible to turn away. Something in his brain yelled at him to run or else he'd be sorry. Elliot agreed with his brain, but his legs didn't obey. He stumbled back a step and then jumped when the Goblin extended a hand—which now looked more like a claw.

"Don't look at him!" the girl in the Elf costume yelled.

Elliot had nearly forgotten about her. Instinct took over, and he swung his sack again at the Goblin, but this time the claw grabbed the sack and tore at it, ripping a big hole. Candy poured out, most of it landing with a *kaplunk* in a big puddle of water that splashed all over the Goblins. The Goblins leapt a foot into the air and screeched as if the water was somehow painful to them. The bubbles melted back into the costumes, though Elliot thought there were holes the size of water droplets in their clothes now.

Without a glance backward, they ran down the street and vanished into the night.

It took a moment for Elliot's heartbeat to return to normal. When he caught his breath, he yelled after them, "Babies!"

If water ruined their costumes so easily, they should've worn something else. He leaned over and picked up a few pieces of candy that weren't too wet. It was the cheap candy, like the kind old women keep in bowls by their TV remotes. There wasn't even enough left to share with his family.

"Sorry about your candy."

Elliot turned to see the girl in the Elf costume speaking to him. She had a small mouth and huge brown eyes. Her hair was thick and hung to her shoulders. Looking at her, Elliot finally understood what a button nose is.

"That's all right," he said. "Someone probably would've stolen it before I got home anyway."

"You have Goblins too?"

He smiled. "Around here we call them bullies."

"Oh." She held out her sack. "Since your candy's ruined, you can have this."

Elliot peeked inside. It was filled with long, green pickles. Dozens of them. Pickle juice leaked from a small hole in her bag and made a smelly puddle on the ground. "Um, no thanks," he said.

"I've got more if you change your mind." She closed her sack and added, "That was really brave, risking your life for me like that."

Maybe that was a bit of an exaggeration, Elliot thought, but he smiled kindly. She was so young, she must've thought the Goblin costumes were real. Poor thing was probably scared half to death. He said, "Nice costume. You're an Elf?"

She puckered her face. "Everyone knows that Elfish ears are short and pointy. I'm a Brownie. My ears are bigger and pointier, see? And Elves are much taller than Brownies. My name is Patches."

"Hi. I'm Elliot." He shifted his feet and found himself staring at her eyes. He'd never seen anyone with eyes that large or that round. "Well, I'd better go home now."

"Okay. Well, thanks for what you did. I won't forget it."

Patches never did forget it, but Elliot's mind was on something entirely different before he even made it home. Maybe

5

he would've remembered if he had known the girl he saved wasn't a human in a Halloween costume, but a real Brownie from her Underworld home.

And as your clever mind also must have guessed, Dear Reader, she was being chased by real Goblins.

Patches went to her Underworld home to tell the other Brownies about her new hero, Elliot Penster. Elliot Penster went home without any Halloween candy. And the Goblins who had ruined his Halloween went home to start a war.

Chapter 2

Where a War Begins

AFTER LEAVING ELLIOT, THE GOBLINS RETURNED TO THEIR Underworld city of Flog. If the name Flog makes you think of a sunny place with green grass and chirping birds, then you are not thinking of the same Flog as where the Goblins live. In the first place, you should have known there's no sun, because Flog is deep underground. Flog gets some light from the glow of the Elves' kingdom, but never quite enough. So it always feels like that hour after the sun goes down but before the moon comes up. Instead of grass and flowers, there are rocks and dirt, and even if a chirping bird somehow finds its way underground, it had better get out quick before it's eaten by a hungry Goblin.

The Goblins weren't hungry at the moment, though. They were busy listening to their two friends describe exactly what Elliot Penster had done to them.

Goblins rarely came face-to-face with a human anymore. That sort of thing used to happen more often a few hundred years ago.

In those days, a Goblin could sneak into a human's home or barn and cause all sorts of wonderful trouble, such as tipping over a lantern or setting the cows loose in the pasture. Meanwhile, the do-good Brownies would work throughout the night repairing holes in shoes or cleaning out fireplaces, always trying to help the humans who did so little for the Brownies in return. It just made the Goblins look even meaner than they actually were.

The Brownies were always careful to leave the home before anyone awakened, but it became quite common for a human to stumble upon a Goblin in the act of causing trouble. When the humans started fighting back, the Goblins had no choice but to join the creatures of the Underworld.

The Goblins still went to the surface now and then, but only if it was really important, such as to chase after a Brownie with a big sackful of pickles. And now that a human had gotten in their way, they crowded into a tight circle to hear the dreadful tale.

If you had actually been sitting with the Goblins in Flog (which I hope is not something you'd ever consider doing, even if you're invited to come; as you've just read, Goblins don't like humans), then you would not have understood what the two Goblins were saying about Elliot. It would have sounded like this: *Arkny flob goopah boohinder human Elliot*, which of course means, "On the surface there is a dangerous human named Elliot" in Flibberish.

All Underworld creatures speak a common language called Flibberish. It is very much like English, except that all the letters to all the words are entirely different. And of course, Flibberish speakers end every conversation by spitting at each other. Many Underworld creatures speak both Flibberish and English, but to make reading easier for you, Dear Reader, whenever the creatures speak in Flibberish, it's been translated to English. If you still can't read it, then you probably don't speak English. Try reading something in Icelandic or pig Latin, and see if one of them is your language instead.

"Tell us about the dangerous human named Elliot!" someone yelled from the crowd.

The larger Goblin, also with the larger vocabulary of at least twenty words, spoke for both of them. "There we were, minding our business"—as they saw it, their business was chasing after an innocent Brownie and her pickles—"when this human ran over to pick a fight with us."

The Flog citizens gasped in horror. Humans were their favorite villains in any story.

"He beat us with a sackful of chocolate candies." More gasping followed this terrible news. "That's right, it was chocolate," the Goblin continued. "We were lucky to escape alive."

The smaller one thrust out his arm, which was covered in welts. "He gave us these too." This had happened when Elliot's sack of candy fell into the water. Water always burns Goblins.

"And he broke all the bones in your face!" a Goblin yelled from the crowd. "You look awful!"

The smaller one rolled his eyes. "No, that's my real face. I always look this way."

There was a slight moment of silence while many Goblins considered that all of them always looked that way. The awkward feeling was soon forgotten as another Goblin in the crowd yelled, "This means war!" It was followed by cheers and plans to go to the surface and begin attacking the humans.

"You'll never win," a Goblin in the back said. His voice sounded like two pieces of sandpaper rubbing against each other. Music to a Goblin's pointy, hairy ears.

Every green Goblin head turned to see the greenest Goblin of all walking to the front of the crowd. His name was Grissel, and he hadn't been seen in public for fifty-five years. He was a decorated hero of the Great Goblin War of the last century, having rescued the entire city of Flog from a human invasion. Goblin children sang songs about him. Goblin females left pickle pies on his doorstep. And Goblin males tried to imitate his fashion sense, although they could never get the rag tied around their waists in just the right way.

By the time Grissel reached the front of the crowd, everyone was silent. He looked the Goblins over for a few moments and then said, "We don't want a war with the humans. There's nothing we want on the surface."

"We want pickles!" a Goblin said.

"And if we kill all the humans, who'll make more pickles for us to steal?" Grissel snarled. "Tell me, what do we like more than pickles?"

"Puppy dogs?" another Goblin said. "Cute little doggies with those sad puppy eyes? They make you just want to hold them and give them a hug."

Grissel stared in disgust and then pointed a finger at the Goblin, who promptly blew up. When the dust settled, Grissel repeated, "I said, what do we like more than pickles?"

– This time there was silence, which wasn't a surprise. Nobody likes to get blown up just for giving a wrong answer.

"We like Brownies," Grissel said. "Maybe a human got involved with us on the surface, but we were after the Brownie girl. If you want to go to war, then we go to war against the Brownies."

A cheer rose throughout the crowd.

So it was, on Halloween night while Elliot lay in his bed feeling bad about having lost his candy, that the Goblins declared war on the Brownies. And the Underworld would never be the same again.

Chapter 3

Where Elliot Sees the World a Whole New Way

THERE ARE MANY CAUSES OF FORGETFULNESS, INCLUDING AT least 236 different diseases, most of which you probably can't pronounce. A good way to know that you don't have any of those forgetting diseases is if you remember that the Brownie child, Patches Willimaker, had decided to keep her eye on Elliot in case the Goblins returned again.

(If you don't remember that, then you might have some form of amnesia. You may have forgotten that you have amnesia, because if you do remember having it, then it probably isn't amnesia at all. Maybe you just weren't reading carefully.)

Three years passed from the night Elliot saved Patches from the Goblins, and all that time, she watched him. Elliot lived in the very small town of Sprite's Hollow, which is about a hundred miles away from anywhere you'd want to be. The weather there was usually just about right for the time of year, except for last July when hail the size of golf balls fell all over town and refused to melt afterward. (Or maybe it was the mini-golf tournament they held around town that day. No one really knows for sure.)

Sprite's Hollow was normally a peaceful town, where cows and chickens outnumbered the people, so it was never hard to find Elliot. A person could run from one end of town to the other in less than twenty minutes, even faster if you were Elliot and were being chased by one of the school bullies.

By the time he was eleven years old, Elliot was so skinny that his normal-size head looked too large for his neck. He had blond hair every summer and brown hair every winter and red hair only once, when he fell into a bucket of mashed beets. His legs had grown in the last year, and his great hope was that the rest of his body would soon grow to match.

Sprite's Hollow was also the kind of town where a kid could get into a lot of trouble with only a little effort. Some kids got into trouble by changing road signs so that travelers who thought they were leaving town actually went back the way they had come. Others snuck into barns and added chocolate syrup to the cow's water, hoping the cow would then produce chocolate milk.

Elliot's trouble was named Tubs Lawless, a kid from up the road who was two years older and two heads taller. He was dumber than a Popsicle and so mean that he jumped every time he looked in the mirror.

Patches had helped Elliot escape trouble with Tubs more than once. Of course, Elliot didn't know that, but she figured over the past three years she'd saved him from at least eighteen bruises, two black eyes, and one note taped to Elliot's back telling the rest of the school to kick him.

Today he was in a bit more trouble than usual. Patches watched Tubs chase Elliot behind Elliot's house. She ducked behind a large elm tree as they raced across the grass on the edge of the woods that bordered Elliot's backyard. The woods were mystery territory. No kid had ever explored them all. Even Elliot could get lost in there. It was rumored that a boy named Mavis had been lost in there for the last twenty-eight years.

No sooner had Elliot run into the woods than a rope grabbed him by the leg and yanked his body up in the air, hanging him upside down. As Tubs got closer, Elliot squirmed to get free, but the rope only tightened.

The rope trap was Elliot's father's idea. He figured it was a good way to catch dinner for the family. It had worked only once before, trapping a skunk that sprayed Elliot's father in the face when he let it go. Now the trap had caught Elliot. Elliot wished he had something to spray Tubs with, like extra-strength bully repellent.

Tubs ran up so close that their noses were almost touching, except of course Elliot's nose was upside down.

"Next time I make you do my homework, you'd better put in the right answers," Tubs said.

"I wrote that Tubs Lawless has pudding for brains," Elliot said, smiling. "I thought that *was* the right answer."

"How should I know?" Tubs asked. "But if it was, then why did the teacher mark it wrong?" After a moment, his eyes widened and he said, "Hey! Pudding for brains—that's an insult!"

Tubs backed up and grabbed a handful of rocks, which he began throwing. Even upside down, Elliot did a pretty good job at avoiding the rocks, but Patches knew Tubs would get in a hit soon. She rolled up her sleeves, preparing to do a little magic to get Elliot down.

"I thought we smelled manure back here," a boy behind Elliot said. "Wait, it's only Tubs."

"Hey, Tubs! Look this way!" another boy said.

Patches turned to see Cole and Kyle, Elliot's six-year-old twin brothers, standing in the yard with a long hose kinked in their hands and a naughty spark in their clear blue eyes. The twins released the kink, and a stream of water shot at Tubs, hitting him squarely in the chest. It knocked him to the ground. He crawled backward, cried for his mommy, then ran away.

"Thanks!" Elliot told his brothers. He didn't often use their names, because he couldn't tell them apart. He sometimes wondered if Kyle and Cole even knew who had which name.

"Our pleasure," answered the twins.

Cole and Kyle loved anything with water. They'd been suspended from kindergarten in their first week for putting a water snake in the boys' bathroom toilet, which got into the pipes and ended up flooding the entire nonfiction section of the school library.

"Mom and Dad are going to be home at any minute!" Elliot's fifteen-year-old sister, Wendy, cried as she barreled into the woods. "Look at this mess. Dinner's going to be burned now." She had white flour in her brown ponytail. That meant bad news. She was cooking.

Elliot and his brothers looked at each other. If the family was lucky, burned was the only problem with Wendy's food. The only reason anyone ever came to eat was because she tricked them by putting a yummy-smelling dessert in the oven to call them.

"I'll cut you down, but I'll be late for work," said sixteen-year-old Reed, the oldest of the Penster children. Reed helped the family by sharing his earnings from working in a fast-food restaurant named the Quack Shack. Nobody thought duck burgers had much of a chance in becoming more popular than plain old hamburgers. They were right. Duck nuggets dipped in barbecue sauce weren't too bad, though. Reed also tried to improve his family's meager food supply by bringing home leftover pickle relish each weekend in case anyone wanted some. No one ever did, and Reed's collection now fit in a jar almost as tall as he was.

Elliot was cut down and the family walked back to their home, a two-story wooden box that leaned in whatever direction the wind blew.

Patches crept out from behind her tree and cradled her head in her hands while she watched them go. It would've been nice to rescue Elliot from Tubs, but that wasn't why she had come here. The Brownies weren't doing well in the war against the Goblins. In this case, "not doing well" meant they were losing in every way possible. She knew that one day the Goblins would decide to come after Elliot too. And she was right.

But as you will see, it didn't happen in the way Patches thought. Elliot just wasn't that lucky.

Chapter
4

Where Queen Bipsy's Spleen Dies. And Everything Else.

DEAR READER, YOU MAY WONDER WHY I HAVEN'T SAID anything yet about a character in this story named Diffle McSnug. The answer is simple. There is no character in this story named Diffle McSnug. As far as I know, nobody named Diffle McSnug has ever existed, so I'm not sure why you'd think I should write about him.

Even if Diffle McSnug existed, he wouldn't have time to sit around in Elliot's story, waiting to do something important. He'd be off on his own adventure, which right about now would involve his diving with sharks to recover some sunken pirate treasure. Only he's almost out of air and the sharks are licking his toes.

I'm sure you'd love to hear how he escapes. It's too bad he never existed, because if he did, I'm sure that would be a fascinating story.

There is someone far more important to write about in this book, and that is the Brownie known as Queen Bipsy. She had just reached the end of her 561st birthday. That would be extremely old for a human, but for a Brownie it was only very old. Her birthday party was the largest in the Brownie Underworld, because she was the queen of the Brownies, and not attending her birthday party was a crime punishable by ten years of hard labor. (Hard labor in the Brownie world is the nonstop eating of chocolate cake…without frosting or a glass of milk, if you can imagine the horror of it.)

Something happened to Bipsy that night as she walked home from her birthday party. From the corner of a cave someone whispered, "Psst, look over here."

Everyone knows that if someone whispers, "Psst, look over here," that definitely means you should *not* look over there. If there were a good reason to look, then they wouldn't have to say "psst" in a whisper.

Queen Bipsy must not have known this, because she did look. From out of the shadows, she saw something bubbling to life. Ripples moved along leathery green skin, and the figure grew in size. Bipsy knew she should run, but all the wiggly juice she had drunk at her party weighed her down. She wanted to run but couldn't move.

Her eyes remained fixed on the monstrous creature, even as it rose above her. The only reason she was still watching it, and not lying dead on the ground from terror, was that she was full up to her eyeballs with wiggly juice, which made her vision blurry.

She could see it well enough to cause her Brownie heart to do a cancan dance inside her chest, though. And she clearly heard the pleasure in the monster's voice as he said, "It took me three years, but I finally got you, Queen Bipsy."

"Queen Bipsy? Are you all right?" A hand touched her shoulder, breaking her trance. The monster that had been in the cave shrank away, and Bipsy turned to face her friend Mr. Willimaker. Even at this late hour and after such a happy party, he still looked morning fresh.

Ordinarily, Brownies don't worry too much about their personal appearance. They usually have a lot of thick hair, which always looks a little gray no matter what color it really is. Their pointy ears often clog with earwax, and their fashion sense stalled a couple of centuries ago. Their only virtue is they bathe often. Just because one lives in the Underworld doesn't mean they have to smell like the Underworld.

Mr. Willimaker was different. His clothes were made by a Pixie tailor and always the latest in Elfish fashion wear. He trimmed his hair and used a bit of magic each morning to get it pointing all the same way. He wore oversize glasses that made his oversized eyes look even bigger and which often slid off his undersized nose.

Most Brownies found it funny that Mr. Willimaker always dressed for success, because success was the last word they would use to describe him. Three years ago, he had run through Burrowsville, the Brownie city, warning everyone to get out while they could. They were being invaded by a strange creature that no doubt planned to kill each and every Brownie in some gruesome way. Mr. Willimaker caused near riots as Brownie families gathered what supplies they could and hurried into the streets.

The mystery was solved by Mr. Willimaker's own daughter, Patches, who recognized the invading creature as a simple field mouse from the surface world. It must have gotten lost and somehow found its way to the Underworld. She scooped the field mouse into her arms and gave it a loving hug. With Queen Bipsy's help they sent it back home.

The Brownies were angry with Mr. Willimaker for several

months at the trouble he had caused. After that, he was laughed at wherever he went. Jokes were written about him, and every time something unusual happened in Burrowsville, the Brownies said, "Maybe it's a mouse attack." If it weren't for the fact that Queen Bipsy was still his friend, Mr. Willimaker would have been laughed out of Burrowsville long ago.

"Are you all right, Queen Bipsy?" Mr. Willimaker asked again.

"No," she answered. "I think I've just been scared to death."

"Pardon me for correcting you, Your Highness, but I notice you're still alive."

Queen Bipsy plumped down on a rock and folded her arms. "Scared *half* to death, then. And I think very soon the other half of me will die."

Mr. Willimaker wondered which half of her had died. Both halves of her body looked equally upset with him. "Could you wait to finish dying until tomorrow?" he asked. "Maybe by tomorrow you'll change your mind and be fine."

"I am the queen, and I'll die when I want to," Queen Bipsy insisted. "I've lived a full life, and besides, I'm pretty sure my spleen just died. You don't seriously expect me to continue living with a half-dead body and no spleen, do you?"

Mr. Willimaker didn't answer. He thought maybe it was a trick question.

Queen Bipsy looked around her. "I need to choose the next ruler of the Brownies. Where's my royal scribe?"

Her royal scribe had been killed in a Goblin attack over a year ago. Maybe her spleen had been in charge of remembering that, before it died.

"I can write for you," Mr. Willimaker offered. He patted his pockets. Somewhere he had a pen—ah, there it was. But paper. He didn't have any paper! The future of the Brownie kingdom was at stake. Why couldn't he find one tiny scrap of paper?

"I don't have all day to die," Queen Bipsy muttered. "Could you hurry it up?"

"Go ahead, Your Highness. Oh! I mean, go ahead and speak. Not go ahead and die. I'll find some paper soon." Mr. Willimaker continued looking through his pockets. He didn't need much. An inch of paper would do.

Queen Bipsy's eyes widened and she gasped. "Too late. I think this is it, the end. I believe this may be my last breath before I die."

Mr. Willimaker gave up his search for paper. Then he did what everyone does when they have an emergency need to write something down. He put the pen to the palm of his hand and said, "I'm ready. What is the name?"

"No, it seems I have another breath." She drew in a slow breath and then added, "There, now this one is probably my last."

Mr. Willimaker leaned forward. "If you could please use that breath, then, to tell me the name of the next ruler..."

"The Brownies will have a king this time."

"A king—yes, that's fine. What's his name?"

"There's only one person—" She paused as she sucked in some air. "You must give him everything necessary to succeed. His name is—"

Then Queen Bipsy's head fell forward onto her chest. Mr. Willimaker sadly bowed his head. She had been a good queen, noble and kind. Her death had come too soon for the Brownies who loved her.

"His name is the following," Queen Bipsy said, tapping him on the shoulder and nearly causing him to jump out of his skin. (You, the reader, may also have nearly jumped out of your skin when you realized the queen was not as dead as Mr. Willimaker had suspected. Studies have shown this very thing happened to twenty-three other readers who failed to fit back into their skin after this point and have had to go skinless since.)

Mr. Willimaker put his pen to his palm. "Yes?"

"No time left to say the name," she whispered. "You must choose him."

Mr. Willimaker tried to point out that it would have been faster to say the name than to have ordered him to choose someone, but it was too late. For when she closed her eyes this time, it was certain she had died, because she didn't spit.

Mr. Willimaker stared at his hand, as if the name should magically appear there. How was he to choose the next king?

For a brief moment he considered writing in his own name, but then he remembered that most Brownies would rather be ruled by a patch of mold than by him. He thought about writing in the name of Fudd Fartwick, the queen's closest advisor, but remembered that Fartwick was cruel and evil, and also a known cheater in the delightful game of buzzball.

If he chose badly, think of how the Brownies would laugh at him then. They'd ask, "How many Brownies does it take to destroy the kingdom? Only one, if it's Mr. Willimaker." Not a funny joke, but the Brownies would laugh about it anyway. No, there had to be a way for him to obey Queen Bipsy's command but still get the Brownies to choose the next king.

He forced his eyebrows together. *Think, Willimaker, think.* His nervous brain simply answered, *no*, and quite rudely too. *Fine*, Willimaker told his brain, *then I'll make this decision without you.*

Dear Reader, even a rude brain is better than no brain at all. If your brain has been rude to you, then you may punish it by watching an entire day of cartoons. But when it has apologized, you must turn off the television and start using it again.

As often happens when one is not using his or her brain to think, Mr. Willimaker came up with an idea certain to end in disaster. The queen had ordered him to choose a name, and he had to obey her command, no matter how strange it was. But if he chose someone who was also strange, it would be impossible for the Brownies to accept him. They'd ignore her wish and choose their own king.

So he chose a king none of the Brownies had ever heard of. In fact, the king wasn't a Brownie at all.

It was a human. A human whose name he knew only because his daughter, Patches, never stopped talking about him. An eleven-year-old boy named Elliot Penster.

Obviously, the Brownies would never allow a human to become their king. They'd ignore Queen Bipsy's will and call for a general election to choose their next ruler.

The plan was clever, foolproof, and perfect in every way but one: the Brownies never ignored Queen Bipsy's will.

Chapter 5

Where Fudd Becomes
Seriously Disappointed

At the news of Queen Bipsy's death, an immediate assembly of all Brownies was called. It was held in Burrow Cave, the only place large enough for all Brownies to meet together. Despite the hundreds of fireflies that flew above them, it was always a little dark in there. That was fine by most Brownies, since it meant they didn't have to look too closely at the Brownie in charge of the meeting, Fudd Fartwick.

Fudd had been Queen Bipsy's advisor for the past four hundred years. At twenty-eight inches, he was taller than most Brownies. His nose was longer than most Brownies' noses and slightly crooked, too, which was okay since it kept most people from noticing his eyes. Fudd had mean eyes. He didn't look at others; he glared at them. If he smiled, it was probably because one of his evil plans had worked. In those happy moments, his eyes shrunk to tiny slits on his stout face. He was the kind of creature whom you wouldn't want to look at very long for fear your eyeballs would burn.

Don't laugh. It's happened before and it's not pretty.

Fudd had one simple, humble wish for his life, which was to become the most powerful creature in the universe. There was only one position for him of greater power with the Brownies, and that was as king. Now that Queen Bipsy had died, he was ready to take the crown for himself.

Fudd had big plans for the Brownies. No more homes in underground tunnels and caverns. No more life as second-rate creatures behind the Elves and Fairies. No more making their living by doing secret chores for the humans. No, it was time for the humans to begin serving *them*.

It would take the help of the Goblins, though he'd have to keep that a secret. Brownies and Goblins weren't the best of friends, mostly because Goblins had spent the past three years trying to kill the Brownies. But Fudd planned to trick the Goblins. As soon as he convinced the Goblins to join him, he could end the war and become the hero of the Brownies— but even more, he'd become the Goblins' king as well.

Fudd smiled. His pointy teeth peeked through his gray lips. *Careful now*, he thought. *Accept the crown first, and then you can make your plans.*

Mr. Willimaker stood to speak to the group. He coughed

several times, because whenever he was nervous, it felt like something was stuck in his throat, like a pumpkin. He hadn't washed his hand with the name of the king on it, although it had become so sweaty that all of the letters had washed together and now said the new king's name was something like "Lnit Prmsln." He didn't know anyone named Lnit Prmsln, so he'd have to go with his first choice.

Dear Reader, if your name happens to be Lnit Prmsln, then in the first place I'm very sorry for you. In the second place, you are not the human Mr. Willimaker intended to become king, so please do not dig a hole hundreds of feet into the earth trying to correct this problem. You'll get very dirty and still won't reach the Underworld. Besides, as you continue reading this story, you'll probably decide that you really don't want to be the king anyway.

Mr. Willimaker cleared his throat again and began to speak, but one of the Brownies yelled out, "Is the scary little mouse coming again, Willimaker? Will the mouse destroy us all this time?"

Mr. Willimaker tried to say that this was not a time for jokes, but everyone was laughing too hard to hear him. His hands sweat even more and blurred the ink so that no one could read it. He was on his own now.

Patches Willimaker walked up to stand beside her father. "Hey!" she yelled. "My dad has something important to say!"

Slowly the noise settled down, and as the eyes of every Brownie in the cave focused on him, Mr. Willimaker was more nervous than ever. With a tremor in his voice, he stated, "Queen Bipsy did many great things for Burrowsville. Except for our troubles with the Goblins, I believe we've always been happy here. Her final wish before she died was to know that our next ruler will bring us the same happiness. Maybe more, if he can end the Goblin war."

A cheer rose in the crowd. Even Fudd cheered, although making the Brownies happy was not in Fudd's secret plans.

Mr. Willimaker continued, "Before she died, Queen Bipsy gave me the name of our next ruler, a king."

Fudd sat taller in his chair. This was his big moment.

"However, those of you who only speak Flibberish may have a problem with this name, because the name is not a Flibberish word."

Fudd shrank in his chair. His name was a Flibberish word, though he didn't like to remind people of that, since it meant "ugly stink face."

Mr. Willimaker continued, "Our next king is a human named Elliot Penster." He paused, waiting for the uproar. At any moment, the Brownies would realize that Queen Bipsy must have made a mistake. Their only action would be to reject Elliot as king and hold an election for their next ruler. Any second now.

There it was! The murmuring began, just as he expected. They were asking each other what the queen might have meant. Maybe she was playing a joke on them and was laughing at them from her grave.

Mr. Willimaker raised a hand, calling for silence. "Now, we all know the queen couldn't really have wanted a human for our king. Therefore, I propose—"

"But the queen knew how Elliot Penster saved me three years ago," said Patches to the entire crowd. "That must be why she chose him. He'll make a great king. I know it!"

Mr. Willimaker stared at his daughter, wondering why he'd ever taught her to speak. She wasn't helping.

"If he's brave enough to save Patches from the Goblins, then maybe he can save all of us," a Brownie in the crowd called out.

"Did I say he's human?" Mr. Willimaker protested. But nobody seemed to hear him.

"I know he can help us," Patches said. "Just yesterday he fought another human that looks like a Troll. A bully named Tubs."

The crowd gasped in shock, although in fact, Brownies think a lot of humans look like Trolls. Patches didn't mention that Elliot almost lost that fight.

Fudd shot from his chair toward Patches. "You mean to tell me that the next king of the Brownies is a human child?"

He turned to Mr. Willimaker. "Are you sure that's the name the queen said? Are you sure what she said didn't sound more like Fudd Fartwick?"

Mr. Willimaker coughed nervously. "Er, no, I think I would've heard that clearly." Now that his brain was speaking to him again, he realized what a terrible idea this had been. He wanted to tell the Brownies that he'd chosen the name himself, but it was too late now. Fudd Fartwick would give him hard labor for lying to all the Brownies and would then take over as king. He couldn't let that happen, even if the lie made his ears turn moldy and sprout grass, which sometimes happens to Brownies who tell lies. He said even more loudly to the crowd, "Elliot Penster is our next king. We must go and tell him the news."

"Hail King Elliot!" the Brownies cheered. "Long live King Elliot!"

Mr. Willimaker became so excited by their cheers that he began to believe he'd done the right thing after all. What he failed to notice was the one Brownie in the entire cavern who was not cheering.

Fudd Fartwick sat back on his chair and folded his arms. The cheer was wrong. King Elliot would not live long. He might not even live until the end of the week.

He needed the Goblins for this. They'd be happy to help. As much as they liked killing any Brownie, they'd like to kill the human king of the Brownies most of all.

Chapter 6

Where Elliot Doesn't Sleep Well

ELLIOT WASN'T THE TYPE TO WAKE UP SUDDENLY IN THE middle of the night, bathed in sweat and afraid for his safety. But his room had never been secretly invaded by creatures from the Underworld before.

"Who's there?" he called out into the darkness. His brother Reed, who shared his room, would've normally answered by tossing a pillow at Elliot and telling him to stop asking strange questions in the middle of the night. But Reed was working at the Quack Shack late tonight. And it wasn't a strange question.

"Are you Elliot Penster?" The voice was higher in pitch than he was used to, as if someone had sucked helium from a balloon before speaking.

"That's me. Who are you?" Elliot switched on the light beside his bed and then jumped back. Two small *things* were on his floor staring up at him, a younger girl and a boy *thing* that might have been her dad, if things had fathers. They were dressed like something out of a fairy tale book and stared at him with wide, hopeful eyes. He didn't think they were trying to be scary, but the fact that they were standing in his room was scary enough.

The boy thing stepped forward. He was dressed in a little suit, and his hair stood out in fewer directions than the girl's. A large pair of glasses slid up and down his nose with the movement of his head. He pushed the glasses up and said, "We're Brownies. Not like the dessert that you eat, but Brownies, the creatures that we hope you don't eat."

Elliot shook his head. "The only brownies I've ever eaten don't talk to me."

Mr. Willimaker smiled at that as the girl nudged him and whispered, "See? I told you he wouldn't eat us."

Mr. Willimaker turned back to Elliot. "We were sent here on behalf of all Brownies. We're friends to you. Do you believe in Brownies?"

"I do now." Earlier that night Elliot would've given a different answer, but it's hard to deny the existence of something that's staring you in the face.

"My name is Mr. Willimaker."

"Oh, well, it's nice to meet you," said Elliot.

Mr. Willimaker pointed to the girl beside him. "This is my daughter, Patches."

Elliot squinted as he looked at her. "I remember you. Halloween three years ago, right?"

"Yes!" Patches seemed pleased to be remembered. At least her ears perked up slightly.

"We live in the Underworld, miles and miles below where we now stand. Not just Brownies there, of course, but also Dwarves and Elves and Pixies—many different creatures. Mostly we keep to ourselves, but I can introduce you around if you'd like."

"Oh, uh, thanks." Elliot waited for the Brownies to say something else, but they didn't. So finally he said, "Is there something I can do to help you?"

The Brownies laughed at that. Elliot pinched his lips together, wondering what the joke was. Then he said, "I don't think that was funny. You came to my room in the middle of the night. I think it's fair for me to ask why."

"Oh, yes," Mr. Willimaker said. "You can ask why, and I'm glad you did. We've come to tell you the good news."

Elliot was suspicious. He didn't know much about Brownies. Maybe their idea of good news was, "Congratulations, your life is about to get a whole lot worse!"

That wasn't exactly it. Mr. Willimaker bowed low. "Congratulations, you are the new king of the Brownies."

It was Elliot's turn to laugh. "Me? That's crazy!"

Mr. Willimaker pressed his thick eyebrows together. "Why? Are you already a king for another Underworld race? The Leprechauns maybe? If it's gold you want—"

"I'm not anyone's king! I'm just a kid. I didn't even know there were Underworld races. Why me?"

Patches stepped forward. "All we know is that right before she died, Queen Bipsy gave my father your name."

"Bipsy? Silly name for a queen."

"You can't pronounce her full name without a lot of spitting and a hard slap to your face," Patches said. "Would you like me to show you?"

"Bipsy's fine," Elliot said quickly and then added, "But I don't want to be king. I've got school tomorrow."

"Just consider being king a sort of homework assignment," Mr. Willimaker said. "There's math homework and English homework. Being our king is like Underworld mythical creature homework."

Elliot folded his arms. "What would I have to do?"

"It's simple. You'll solve whatever little problems come up, such as who gets the potato if it grows across two garden patches."

"You'll sentence prisoners to hard time," Patches said.

"And drink all the turnip juice you want," Mr. Willimaker said.

"And end the war with the—" Patches began before her father clamped a hand over her mouth.

Elliot tilted his head. "What's that last one?"

Mr. Willimaker looked at his feet and mumbled, "Oh, nothing, there's just this little…"

"I can't hear you," Elliot said. "Could you speak louder?"

Mr. Willimaker coughed. "There is this small matter of a war, between the Goblins and Brownies. Well, it's not really a war, since we don't know how to fight back. So it's more like we just wait around to get killed. Most of us are tired of waiting around to be killed, so we hope as king you'll help us end all of that trouble."

Elliot looked at Patches. "Those kids in the Goblin suits three years ago—"

She nodded. "Yep. Real Goblins."

"Figures. They ruined all my candy, you know." Elliot scratched his chin and asked, "Aren't Brownies the creatures that have to do nice things for humans, like if we leave you a job to do?"

"We don't *have* to do anything," Patches said. "We choose to help *if* we like the gift the human leaves for us."

"Yes, but if I were your king, you'd have to do a job just because I ordered you to, right?"

The two Brownies looked at each other. "Well, yes. But we only work at night," Mr. Willimaker said.

Elliot looked over at the clock in his room but then remembered there was no clock in his room, because his family had sold it last week to buy bread. So instead he looked out the window. "Night's almost over, so you'll have to hurry. I'll make you a deal. My Uncle Rufus is getting out of jail tomorrow, and we're having a welcome home dinner. If you can have a nice dinner ready for my family, then I'll be your king."

Uncle Rufus was the oldest man in town who still had all his teeth. He stayed young by eating healthy, taking walks along Main Street, and unfortunately, by stealing shiny things. He claimed he always meant to buy the items, but he had memory problems. The police didn't believe that, but Elliot did. After all, Uncle Rufus often forgot Elliot was a boy and brought him shiny earrings every birthday.

The Brownies smiled. Mr. Willimaker said, "That's it? Make your family dinner? But it's so simple."

"You say that now. Wait until you see my family's empty cupboards." Elliot figured he'd win no matter what. Either he'd get a nice meal tomorrow night or else he wouldn't have to be the Brownie king and end a war with the Goblins. And even if he were king, he'd just do what they wanted for a few weeks and then give the job to someone else.

"Your wish is our command," Patches said, bowing.

"There's one more thing," Mr. Willimaker said. "We have one simple but very important rule. You can't tell anyone that we exist. If you do, you'll never see us again."

"Never?"

Patches nodded. "We don't appear to humans who tell our secrets."

"I won't tell," Elliot said. He was pretty good with secrets. His parents still didn't know where he had buried the glass vase he'd accidentally broken over the summer.

After the Brownies left, Elliot lay back on his bed, wondering what would happen tomorrow. Him, a king? He had holes in the knees of most of his pants. The fanciest thing he owned was the rusty horn on his bike (not counting the earrings Uncle Rufus stole for him). And he still had to take orders from his sister when she said to eat his vegetables, no matter what color they were. Somehow he didn't feel like a king. But Mr. Willimaker seemed sure that Queen Bipsy had chosen him, so he fell asleep with a smile on his face.

Most readers of this story agree that Elliot probably wouldn't have fallen asleep if he knew that hiding in the corner was a third Brownie named Fudd Fartwick. And Fudd Fartwick was watching the sleeping boy, deciding it wouldn't be hard at all for a small band of Goblins to kill him.

Chapter 7

Where Fudd Plays with Fire

By the time the first morning rays peeked over the horizon, Fudd Fartwick had thought of at least fourteen ways in which he might kill Elliot. Fifteen ways, if he counted making Elliot play out in the warm autumn sunshine for a few hours. On second thought, perhaps that was only deadly to a Brownie. Brownies could tolerate a little sun, but they didn't like it, which is why they did their work at night.

Fudd snapped his fingers to take him back to the Underworld, vanishing from Elliot's bedroom only about twenty seconds before Elliot awoke. Elliot awoke because he smelled something unusual in his home: hot breakfast. Unless his ears were playing a cruel joke on him, that was definitely bacon sizzling downstairs, and he was certain he detected the quiet *thup* of toast popping up. He'd asked the Brownies to provide his family with dinner. Was it possible they would provide food for the entire day? He jumped out of bed and ran from his room so quickly that he didn't notice the tiny dart stuck into his bed, not four inches from where his head had been.

The poison dart had been Fudd's first idea. But Fudd wasn't a good shot, and he'd only brought one poison dart with him. Rule number eight in *The Guidebook to Evil Plans* clearly stated, "Always have a backup plan in case your first try misses (page 24)." Fudd had forgotten that rule tonight, but he wouldn't let himself forget again.

He poofed himself directly to Flog, the Goblin city. Fudd was fully aware that the last Brownie to accidentally poof himself into Flog came home with most of his fingers bitten off, but Fudd was no ordinary Brownie, and he had not come here by accident.

Fudd was—until yesterday—the closest advisor to Queen Bipsy, making him the second most powerful Brownie in the Underworld. By the end of today, he planned to be the closest advisor to Grissel, leader of the Goblins, and the newest secret enemy of King Elliot.

The Goblins stared at him with hunger in their black eyes, and Fudd shuddered. The eyes alone wouldn't be so bad, but combined with their jagged teeth and mossy green skin, Goblins were never a pretty sight. It had been over a thousand years since a Goblin won the Miss Underworld Beauty Pageant. As the story went, the only reason she won was because the other entrants were literally scared to death of her. Being the only living contestant by the end of the show, the crown was hers.

The Goblins were at that moment fighting over bites of an enormous pumpkin. Fudd hoped they would be so full of pumpkin that they wouldn't want to eat him. But he knew better. Goblins were always hungry for Brownies.

Dear Reader, I'm sure you can understand this. While we humans don't eat Underworld creatures, most humans feel there is always room for one more bite of the chocolate cake–like dessert known as a brownie. For Goblins, it's not much different.

Fudd raised an arm, showing them his gold ring, a sign that he was a royal advisor. They wouldn't attack him if they saw it. He hoped. In his most commanding voice, he said, "Take me to Grissel."

No one answered. Even for a Goblin, it's not polite to speak with a full mouth. But they pointed to a crooked, gray house at the top of a crooked, gray hill. Fudd thanked them, kicked at a Goblin child who was at that moment gnawing on his leg, and then made his way up to the house.

As it turned out, Grissel was sitting on a rock in front of the house, as if he'd expected Fudd to come. Over the past few years, he'd grown meaner-looking than when Fudd had last seen him. Like most other Goblins, his clothing was unimaginative and in need of serious repair. Fudd tilted his head toward Grissel, not a deep bow as you'd have to give a royal, but still a show of respect.

"I knew you'd come, Fartwick," Grissel said, licking his lips. "Your smell arrived faster than you did."

Fudd wanted to point out that Goblins—who avoided water because of the welts it left on their skin—were the worst smelling of any Underworld creature (except perhaps for Trolls, who often create their own swimming holes with how much they sweat). But rather than insult someone who had the ability to swallow him whole, he said, "It's an honor to speak with you, Grissel."

Grissel didn't act like he was honored to speak with Fudd. Instead, he looked at Fudd like he wasn't sure whether to eat him headfirst or feet first.

"What do you want with the Goblins?" Grissel finally asked.

Fudd's eyes narrowed. "Maybe you heard about our queen. She died the other night. Something scared her to death."

Grissel couldn't hold back the smile on his face. "I did hear that. I planned to send flowers, but since it was me who scared her to death, I thought flowers would seem insincere."

A shiver ran up Fudd's spine. "Er, yes, good reasoning. Well, shortly before Queen Bipsy's death, she gave the name of our next king."

"And you're mad because it wasn't you."

Fudd shook his head. "No, I'm mad because it's a human boy. His name is Elliot Penster."

"Why should the Goblins care?"

"Because you know this boy. Do you remember Halloween three years ago?"

Most Goblins have trouble remembering anything from three minutes ago, but deep in the cobwebs of Grissel's mind, he did recall the night when a human got between two of his Goblins and their Brownie dessert. Grissel's shriveled heart pounded in his bony chest like it had in the good old days. The war with the Brownies had become boring lately. They never tried to fight back anymore. So there was no challenge, no glory. A human sounded more interesting. Especially a human who had already interfered with the Goblins once before. His pointed ears warmed as he thought of how he'd tell the Goblins about their new enemy.

"And you say this boy is the king of the Brownies now?" Grissel asked.

"If he agrees to be king, he'll be a ruler in the Underworld!" Fudd said. "Do you want that?"

Grissel leaned forward and thought about Fudd's question. It took a very long time, because Goblins aren't that smart, but Fudd waited patiently. Finally, Grissel looked up at him. "No, the Goblins do not want any humans ruling here, but especially not the human named Elliot Penster."

Fudd smiled and took a seat on a smaller rock near Grissel. Like everything else in Flog, the rock was pointy and made sitting very uncomfortable, so he stood again and rubbed his bottom. Then he said, "I'm going to Elliot's home tonight. I'll let him know what dangerous things can happen to an Underworld king. In the meantime, I need you to cause a little trouble down here."

Of all causes that Goblins support, trouble is their favorite. Grissel's face widened into a crooked smile, and he said, "How can we help?"

Chapter 8

Where Patches Gets Out of School Early

FUDD AND GRISSEL MADE AN UNUSUAL TEAM. IT WAS TRUE they shared a deep, driving thirst for power. It was also true that each had gained his power through a talent for being the scariest of his kind.

But the tales of how they rose to power are very different.

Fudd had been born to the two nicest Brownies in all of Burrowsville. It's true. His parents even received an award for niceness once, although they hid it away so it didn't make other Brownies feel bad. They taught Fudd always to act politely and speak kindly. They taught him so well that through most of his first thirty-eight years of childhood, he didn't know what a mean Brownie was. The first time he heard someone sneeze and not say "excuse me, please," he ran home crying.

Grissel had not been born to the nicest Goblins in all of Flog. In fact, his father tried to eat him for Christmas dinner every year, which sort of ruined the holidays.

One day in school, Fudd kindly asked a Brownie girl if he could have a turn on the swing. He'd waited in line for five whole hours, but every time he got to the front of the line, someone else would push ahead of him. He'd never gotten a turn on the swing, no matter how many times he asked. Not even once.

"You can't make me," the Brownie girl told him with a sneer.

So Fudd pulled out the strongest weapon he had, the one thing his parents said would always work. Very politely, he said, "Please."

His parents were wrong, however. It didn't work. She laughed and kept on swinging.

I'm sure you know, Dear Reader, that Fudd could stand up for himself and still be a kind person. You could probably think of at least three ways in which Fudd could solve this problem. Fudd couldn't even think of one.

Something changed in Fudd that day. The swing didn't matter. Saying "please" didn't matter. All that mattered was power, so that no one, ever again, would tell him that he couldn't make them do what he wanted. One day that girl on the swing would see how powerful he'd become, and then she'd be sorry for not sharing. He would work his way up in power until he was king of Burrowsville. No—king of the Underworld.

Unlike Fudd, Grissel had never gone to school. No schools existed in Flog, because there was nobody smart enough to teach in one. Unless you count the Flog Academy of Fear-Making, in which Goblins practiced the art of causing fear in others. With his natural talents, Grissel quickly growled, attacked, and clawed his way to the top of his class. He was especially good at blowing things up. In fact, for graduation he blew up the Flog Academy of Fear-Making. The academy wanted to give him a medal for having done such a good job at it, but the medal had been inside the school and also blasted to smithereens. Grissel's father was so proud, saying that next Christmas he could eat at the table instead of being eaten on the table.

Not long after that, the humans opened a mining operation that caused them to dig very deep into the earth. Their drills came close to Flog, too close. The Goblins tried everything they could think of to stop the humans, such as kicking in their tunnels and breaking their drills with rocks. Nothing worked. They just made wider tunnels and stronger drills.

One day Grissel decided it was time to stop the humans once and for all. He led a group of Goblins to the surface one night. They blew a giant hole into the earth and drove all the human machines into the hole. With another explosion,

Grissel buried the machines. The humans decided the ground wasn't stable enough for mining, and all drilling stopped. Grissel was a hero.

He had lived a quiet life in Flog until three years ago when that human boy, Elliot Penster, stopped the Goblins from catching the Brownie, Patches Willimaker. Then he knew it was time to be the Goblins' hero once again. He had led them in a war against the Brownies ever since.

Fudd wanted to be the Brownies' hero. He had spent his life trying to become the most powerful of all Brownies. It cost all of his gold to buy the only existing copy of *The Guidebook to Evil Plans*, which clearly stated, "Commit to your beliefs. No super villain ever rose to the top by doing things halfway (page 2)." Queen Bipsy had stood in his way before. Now it was King Elliot who kept him down.

But Fudd couldn't kill King Elliot on his own. Very deep inside, Fudd knew that just wasn't nice. And by nature, Brownies are usually peaceful creatures. But now that he and Grissel had joined together, things were different. With Fudd's superior mind and Grissel's ability to create trouble, Fudd was sure that nothing could stop them.

"If we're going to get Elliot, then we need to know more about humans," Fudd said to Grissel. "There's only one Brownie smart enough to help us. Patches Willimaker."

"Where is she now?"

"Probably in school," Fudd said. "Probably in room twelve on the fourth row, probably coming back from lunch right about now." Grissel stared at him, but Fudd just shrugged. "What? It's just a guess. How would I know?"

Oddly enough, that was exactly where Patches was when the Goblins showed up.

Patches was just about to raise her hand and answer the teacher's question about her favorite food when her teacher cried out in fear and pointed to the back of the classroom.

Patches knew what was happening just by the nasty smell that she'd detected. *Goblins.* Luckily, the school had conducted a Goblin drill only last week, and she remembered what to do. She jumped to her feet and yelled to her classmates, "Don't look at them. Just run!"

Despite her own warning, Patches snuck a look behind her. Three Goblins had come. They looked confused by all the Brownies who were frantically running in every direction. Confused and hungry.

The smelliest of them all focused a stare on her, and his eyes narrowed. Patches ran for the fish tank at the back of the room. She scooped the one fish inside into a cup and then pulled the rest of the tank over on its side. Water splashed across the ground, making instant mud. Two of the Goblins backed away from the water. As long as the ground was wet, they wouldn't touch her.

Two Goblins? Wait, where was the third?

"Gotcha!" a voice said, and as she looked up a claw reached down from the ceiling and snatched her off her feet. A Goblin lifted Patches into the air, hanging her by her pants. She squirmed and kicked but could not make him let go.

"Put me down or you'll be sorry," Patches said.

The Goblin laughed as he crawled across the ceiling. "What could a weak Brownie ever do to make a Goblin be sorry?"

Patches had no answer for that. And she had bigger problems right now than coming up with a clever reply. Like staying alive for the next five minutes.

Usually when Brownies are afraid, they get very quiet and worry until they have upset tummies. Sometimes they get loud hiccups and can't stop sneezing. When Patches was afraid, she talked. Even more than usual. "I didn't know Goblins could crawl on the ceiling," Patches said to the Goblin who carried her. "How do you do that?"

"I'm not sure, but it's pretty fun," Grissel replied.

"If I could crawl on the ceiling, then I'd just live there all the time. I'd do everything on the ceiling except drink from a cup, because the water would just spill out onto the floor."

"I wouldn't know," Grissel said. "Goblins don't drink water. Now be quiet, because all this talking makes it harder to steal you." Keeping hold of Patches, he nimbly dropped to the ground. "Let's go," he said to the other Goblins. Then he threw Patches over his shoulder and walked away.

If you've never been carried over a Goblin's shoulder, you should know that it's as uncomfortable as it sounds. Goblin shoulders are made of muscles so hard you might as well be carried by a rock, so even a thick layer of Brownie fat isn't enough to protect against them. And poor Patches didn't have as much fat as the usual Brownie, since her favorite food was carrots.

"Where are we going?" Patches asked.

"Flog. You'll be our guest there for a while. And don't even think about poofing yourself away. I order you not to do it."

Patches frowned. Most Goblins wouldn't have remembered to do that. She tried another idea. "I've got a bad case of burps. If you eat me, you'll get them too."

"I'm not going to eat you. We have some questions for you."

"About what?"

"About how to get rid of your human king."

"He's my friend. I won't help you do that."

Grissel laughed. "Yes, you will. You will, or else I'll stop your burping for good."

Which normally would've been a good thing. But something told Patches that Grissel had meant what he said in the very worst way possible.

Where There Are Pickles,
Pie, and Brownies

ELLIOT HAD SPENT THE ENTIRE DAY THINKING ABOUT WHETHER he wanted to become the Brownie king. He thought about it during recess when he should have been watching the ball that smacked him in the face. He thought about it during lunch when he should have told Dorcas, the lunch lady, he most definitely did *not* want lima beans on his tray. And he thought about it during science when the teacher asked what he'd get if he mixed hydrogen and oxygen. Elliot had said, "Brownies." He was given detention on Friday for that.

What Elliot finally decided was that he was no good at making decisions. If he couldn't decide whether to become king, how could he possibly make decisions for the Brownies? And he didn't like the idea of fighting a war with the Goblins. He remembered the Goblins he'd met on Halloween three years ago, the way their skin had boiled and bubbled. He'd been lucky that the water splashing on them made them leave, because he was sure they were getting ready to do something bad. Ever since that night, Elliot didn't like scary movies so much. He'd already seen the real thing.

But would he really say no to being king just because he was scared? Elliot could handle scary. After all, Tubs Lawless was scary. Even Tubs's parents were afraid of him. They bought him a new toy every single day as a reward for not burning down their house. He usually took the old toys to school and threw them at Elliot.

Elliot was good at dodging the little things, like electronic games and action figures. It was harder to avoid the bigger things, like Tubs's bicycle.

Just thinking of it now gave Elliot a shudder.

But there was more. Elliot knew he could fight back. He remembered the time when Tubs had tried to push him off the bus. Elliot had tripped him, and Tubs fell face first into the mud. It had been one of the best moments of Elliot's life. Maybe winning a war against the Goblins would feel just as good.

King of the Brownies, how hard could it be? They certainly lived up to his order to provide food for the day. Crispy bacon, toast with homemade jelly, and fluffy pancakes were waiting for him when he came downstairs that morning. Mother happily accused Father of making it for the family as a surprise. Father looked confused, but he didn't deny it. And if dinner was as good as breakfast, then from now on he could eat like...well, he could eat like a king.

That night, Elliot stared at his table loaded with roast beef, steamed carrots, and fresh bread. He would be king for anyone who could cook like this.

Beside him, Kyle reached a hand out to take a slice of bread, but Wendy pushed it away. "Not until Mom and Dad get back with Uncle Rufus."

"They wouldn't care if we started eating. Uncle Rufus is used to cold jail food. We're not." Reed leaned closer to the table so he could smell the food better.

"I'll bet jail food is a lot better than Wendy's food," Cole grumbled.

Wendy looked as if she was thinking about getting mad. Then she shrugged and said, "I guess it wouldn't hurt if we started eating. Just eat slowly so it looks like we waited longer."

Reed, Kyle, and Cole dug into the food so quickly that there was no room for Elliot to dish up his plate. He wanted to stand on his chair and tell them the food was really his because the Brownies made it. But even if he did, everyone was so busy eating that they wouldn't have heard him. Finally, he sat back on his chair to wait for a turn.

"We're home!" Father announced as they came through the doorway. He was carrying a big sack full of Uncle Rufus's belongings from jail. Elliot didn't think his uncle would bother to unpack. As soon as he stole again, he'd just need to pack up to go back to jail.

"Come say hello to Uncle Rufus," Mother said as she walked in. Then she stopped and put her hands on her hips. "Don't you think you should have waited for us before eating?"

"I told them to wait," Wendy said with a mouthful of bread.

"I see that Elliot waited," Father said. "Such a polite boy."

Elliot didn't tell his parents that waiting wasn't his choice. If they wanted to think he was polite, then he didn't want to disappoint them.

Uncle Rufus stopped in the doorway and looked around. "Where's my family?" It sounded as if he were really asking. Maybe his eyes were getting worse.

This time, Elliot beat the others to be first in line to hug his uncle. "We're glad you're home," he said.

Uncle Rufus studied Elliot's face. "Something's different about you. You're standing taller."

"Nobody beat me up today," Elliot said.

"Well, isn't that nice," Uncle Rufus said, patting Elliot on the head.

As Elliot's parents helped Uncle Rufus get seated at the table, Mother stared at all the food and asked, "Where did this meal come from?"

"We know Wendy didn't cook it, because she didn't need to trick us with dessert to get us to come," Kyle said.

Cole laughed and added, "And we know Dad didn't cook it, because this is real food, not something Dad trapped with his rope outside."

"Don't be silly," Father said. "I've never gotten that trap to work. Except for that skunk, of course, which I still say would have tasted fine if it didn't smell so skunkish."

"Well, wherever dinner came from, it's the best way to welcome Uncle Rufus home from jail," Mother said.

Uncle Rufus smiled at his family, and the wrinkles around his eyes folded together. "Speaking of jail, I forgot that I brought each of you a gift." He reached into his jacket pocket and pulled out shiny key chains for Father, Reed, Kyle, and Cole, and earrings for Mother, Wendy, and…"Oh dear,

Elliot. I forgot you wouldn't want earrings, your being a boy and all."

Elliot didn't want the earrings or the key chains. "Stealing is against the law, Uncle Rufus."

"It still is?" Uncle Rufus sighed. "Well, you never know. Laws are always changing."

Mother held out her hand, and everyone passed their gifts to her to return to the store. "Elliot's right, Rufus. Besides, you can see this wonderful meal, and we have all our family together. There's nothing more we need."

Wendy cleared her throat. "Mom, you have to tell Kyle and Cole to stop playing with the hose in the yard."

"Why?" Mother asked.

"Tattletale," the twins grumbled in unison.

Wendy continued, "They pulled the hose all the way into the woods today and let the water run until it made a swamp back there."

Mother gave Kyle and Cole the "we're going to have a talk about this later" look and then turned to the rest of the family. "Who saved room for dessert?"

Elliot had forgotten to save any room for dessert, but it was his favorite, cherry pie. There was probably room behind his eyeballs. "I want a big piece." He handed his dinner plate to Wendy, who was clearing the table. Then he winced as something kicked his foot.

"Stop it," he said to Kyle. Or Cole. He wasn't sure which one was sitting next to him.

"Stop what?" Kyle or Cole said. Elliot stared at both of them. It was Kyle. Probably.

Something kicked him again. He quickly looked under the table to catch the guilty person and then realized it wasn't a person at all. It was a Brownie...well, two Brownies: Mr. Willimaker and another mean-looking one he hadn't met yet.

Mr. Willimaker bowed at him, and after a very long sigh, so did the other.

"What?" Elliot hissed. "I'm eating."

"This is an emergency," Mr. Willimaker said. "You must come with us."

"Where?"

"To the Brownie Underworld."

"Not before dessert. And I'm not going to anyone's Underworld. My mom doesn't want me out of the house after dark."

"Then where can we talk?"

"Up in my room. Ten minutes."

Elliot glanced up just as his mother set a thick slice of warm cherry pie in front of him. "Who were you talking to under the table?" Mother asked.

"Oh, uh, my feet."

She blinked. "You were talking to your feet?"

"Nothing wrong with that," Father said. "I used to talk to my feet all the time as a boy. They're very good listeners."

"As long as your feet don't talk back," Rufus agreed. "That's when you should worry."

Elliot didn't have time to worry about whether his feet would ever talk to him. He wanted to enjoy every bite of his pie. Now he had to hurry and eat it so he could see what the Brownies wanted.

Ten minutes later he ran to his room and shut the door. Mr. Willimaker and the other Brownie stood on his bed. They bowed again.

"You don't have to do that," Elliot said. "I haven't even agreed to be your king yet."

"You probably won't want to either, when you hear our news," the mean-looking Brownie said. His thin lip curled in a sneer, and his bushy gray eyebrows were pushed so tightly together Elliot could barely see his eyes. Elliot had seen that same expression on Tubs's face plenty of times and knew what it meant. For some reason, this Brownie didn't like him.

"Who are you?" Elliot asked.

Mr. Willimaker bowed. "Forgive me, Your Highness—er, Your Elliot-ness, er, Elliot. This is Fudd Fartwick. He was the closest advisor to Queen Bipsy and will be your advisor now. He came with me to share some terrible news."

Elliot sat on his bed beside the Brownies. "What news?"

"The Goblins are causing trouble again. They came into Burrowsville, the Brownie city."

"Tell me about the Goblins," Elliot said. "Why are they at war with you?"

"At war with *us*," Fudd corrected. "If you're the king, then they're at war with you too."

Elliot sighed. "Okay. Why are they at war with *us*?"

Mr. Willimaker coughed and then muttered, "It seems we taste good."

"Huh?" Elliot asked.

"We taste good. To Goblins. And we're not strong enough to fight back, so it's very easy for them to come get one of us every now and then."

Elliot leaned against his headboard. He would've leaned right into Fartwick's poison dart, except Fartwick had already taken it back when Mr. Willimaker wasn't looking. It was now stuffed into his pants, making it uncomfortable for him to sit. Not to mention sort of dangerous.

"I don't know anything about Goblins," Elliot said. "I don't know how to fight them, and I don't know how to help the Brownies win any war. I can't be your king."

"Good choice," Fudd said, maybe a little too quickly. "You don't want to mess with Goblins. They're nasty creatures."

"Will they hurt humans?"

Fudd shrugged. "The Goblins scared Queen Bipsy to death. I don't know if they can scare humans to death or not, but I'm sure they'll try. There is also perhaps the slightest possibility that they'll blow you up. It's a Goblin specialty. I assume you're against that idea."

Elliot was very much against the idea of being blown up. He liked all his body parts attached to him just the way they were. He wasn't too fond of being scared to death either.

Fudd continued, "Besides, I'm sure we could find someone else who could do a much better job. Maybe a Brownie who's already been a close advisor or something to someone important, like a queen."

"Like you?" Mr. Willimaker said with a scowl.

Fudd angrily folded his arms. "You have to admit it's very odd that Queen Bipsy chose a human to replace her when she could have picked me. She must have lost her senses before she died."

"Her senses were working fine," Mr. Willimaker insisted.

"I want to know more about the Goblins," Elliot said.

Mr. Willimaker slowly shook his head. "There's something I haven't told you about the Goblins coming to Burrowsville. They took my daughter, Patches, with them. I think it's because she knows more about humans than anyone else in the Underworld. I need your help to get her home."

"Your daughter must have been in the wrong place at the

wrong time," Fudd grumbled. "Where was she? Somewhere dangerous, no doubt."

"In school," Mr. Willimaker said.

"Aha!" Fudd exclaimed. "What sort of loving father would send his child to school? You might as well have sent Patches to try her luck in Demon Territory."

"Will the Goblins hurt her?" Elliot asked.

"I sent them a large jar of pickles. Goblins love pickles, the only thing they like more than us. I hope they'll eat the pickles instead of Patches." Mr. Willimaker's lower lip trembled a little, and then he placed his chubby hand on Elliot's arm. "It doesn't matter how you became king. The important thing is that we need you and that if you don't help us, we will lose." He lifted the corner of a blanket to reveal something that looked like a wide and pointy gold bracelet. It was a crown. Several oval jewels were set around the base with a fat ruby in the center. "Will you accept the job?"

Elliot smiled and picked up the crown. It was too small for his head, so he held it between his fingers and nodded. "Yes, Mr. Willimaker. I am Elliot Penster, and as of today, I am king of the Brownies."

Chapter 10

Where Patches Is Tempted by Turnip Juice

DEAR READER, BEING THE SMART PERSON YOU ARE TO HAVE read so far into this book, I'm certain that you enjoy every minute of your day at school. However, you might have one or two friends who sometimes complain that school is boring.

You might tell them that even though they get bored at times, it happens to be much better than being carried away from school into the Goblin city of Flog, like Patches Willimaker was.

Patches had spent the rest of her day in a very deep hole that was made of rock, so she could not tunnel through it. The hole had a dirt floor that was so hard she couldn't write her will into it with her finger, and no windows, so the only thing to look at was rock. Although even if there were a window, it would still only show her more rock. Patches had tried to poof away several times, even though Grissel had ordered her not to. Since she was Grissel's prisoner, she should have known poofing wouldn't work.

Patches also knew that at any minute the Goblins would come and try to get information about the human, but Patches had a plan. She wouldn't help them hurt King Elliot, no matter what.

Her stomach growled at her, which she thought was a little rude, because there was nothing she could do to get more food. Before she could ask her stomach to stop complaining, a rope ladder swung down. "It's Grissel," growled a voice from up on top of her hole. "If you want to live, then you'll cooperate with me."

"Actually, you'd better cooperate with me," Patches said. "I've got a big Flibberish test in school next week. If I'm not back to take the test, then my teacher will come here to give it to me, and trust me, you don't want that. She'll make you take it too."

Grissel was quiet for a moment, and Patches wondered if he'd gone away. Then he called down, "In that case, you'd better tell me what I need to know. I have a question for you."

"No, thanks," Patches called up. "I'm pretty busy right now. Can you come back later?"

"If you help me, I'll let you go."

Patches shook her head. "You don't have to let me go. I plan on escaping by myself."

"I have carrots," Grissel said. "Fat, juicy carrots boiled in turnip juice."

Carrots. That changed everything.

Anyone who's ever eaten carrots boiled in turnip juice will understand why Patches's mouth began watering. Close your eyes and imagine the yummiest dessert ever. Now pour turnip juice all over it and let the flavors blend together. Mmmmm. It was a good thing Patches already had a plan to help King Elliot, because who knows what she might have done otherwise.

This wasn't the first time turnip juice had been used to lure a Brownie. Hundreds of years ago, human mothers could leave a bucket of turnip juice outside with a large pile of laundry. By morning, the turnip juice was gone and the laundry was clean and hung to dry on the line. The mothers thought their plan was pretty clever, but the Brownies always knew they had the better end of the bargain.

"Give me the carrot," Patches said. The delicious smell was becoming too much for her. "I'll tell you anything you want to know."

Grissel sent the carrot down tied to a string, but it was just out of reach, even when Patches jumped for it. Her short, chubby legs were usually one of her prettiest features, but what a curse they were at this moment!

"Okay, I give up. What's your question?" Patches finally asked.

"How can the Goblins defeat King Elliot?"

Patches was quiet for a moment. Then she smiled. "You can't," she said. "Humans aren't like Brownies. Humans don't wait around for something to come and eat them. They fight back. They defend themselves."

"We can scare the human to death," Grissel said. "He can't defend against that."

Patches yawned loudly. "That old trick? I remember the good old days when Goblins were more creative in how they got humans. Do you think humans would've written all those fairy tales about you if you were as boring then as you are now?"

Grissel sighed. Things *had* been a little ordinary lately. "There's a lot more that we can do," he called down to Patches. "We have magic. And really sharp claws."

"He expects you to use your magic and your claws. If you want to get him, you have to do what he doesn't expect." Patches didn't actually think Elliot was expecting anything to happen, especially magic and claws.

"Oh, I have a plan he won't expect," Grissel said. "It's foolproof."

"That's what I've been trying to tell you! He expects the foolproof plan already. That's how humans are. If you really want to get King Elliot, you have to use your *not* foolproof plan."

Grissel sat back and rubbed his meaty hand along his prickly jaw. In a very strange way, that made sense to him. "Our not foolproof plan, yes, that's clever."

Grissel lowered the string to give Patches the carrot and then called to the other Goblins. They came quickly, pushing into a tight circle around Grissel and standing so closely together that it was hard to tell where one green Goblin started and the other ended. Patches pressed her body against the wall of her hole, because if one Goblin fell in, a bunch of them would fall with him, and she didn't want to be crushed.

"I need three of you to come with me right away. We're going to outsmart the king by not outsmarting him at all!"

That didn't make sense to any of the Goblins, but they cheered anyway. After all, Grissel had never led them wrong before.

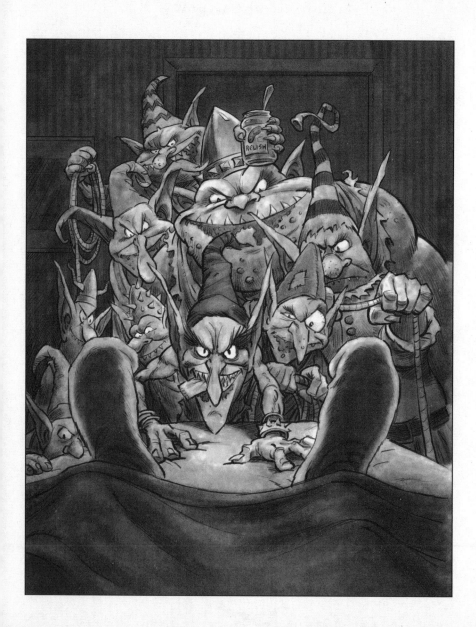

Chapter 11

Where Grissel Tries the Not Foolproof Plan

THE MOON WAS HIGH IN THE SKY WHEN THE GOBLINS poofed themselves into Elliot's room. There were two beds on opposite sides of the room. One bed was empty, but several packets of pickle relish were on top of the blankets. The Goblins fought over them until Grissel won. This was because he knew the other Goblins' ticklish spots, and for a Goblin, getting tickled just isn't funny. He stuffed the packets into his mouth and swallowed them whole.

Then Grissel pointed to the other bed. Something in the shape of a human was underneath the blankets. Dangling on the bedpost was his crown. King Elliot was within their reach.

The Goblins smiled at each other, proud to be a part of the war against the human king. Grissel smiled the widest, unaware of the packet of pickle relish stuck between his pointy front teeth. This was almost too easy for a Goblin of his talents. In just a few minutes, he could return and tell Fudd Fartwick their Brownie king was no more.

Grissel knew exactly what Fudd's next move would be. He'd hurry back to Burrowsville and tell the Brownies the sad news about Elliot. Maybe he'd pretend to cry over Elliot's death for a minute or two, and then he'd wipe away his fake tears and declare himself king. It would be perfect.

Except Fudd wouldn't be able to do any of that, because the hole Grissel had tunneled out for Fudd was even deeper than the one Patches was in. With Fudd out of the way and no Brownie king to lead them, it would be a simple thing to defeat the Brownies once and for all. He smacked his thin lips just thinking about his delicious victory.

Grissel handed some rope to the other Goblins, who climbed up on Elliot's bed. They rolled him around in his blanket, surprised that the human could sleep so deeply. They tied the rope in a double knot, then a triple knot, then finally, in the never-before-untied four-way knot. There was no going back now.

They lifted his body into the air and tossed it toward Grissel, who already had a large trunk at the foot of Elliot's bed open and empty. Elliot could wait in the trunk until they had a chance to get rid of him properly. Most of him landed inside the trunk, except for his legs, which fell limp onto the floor.

Grissel walked over and kicked at Elliot's legs. They rustled softly, something Grissel didn't think human legs normally did. Then his lip curled in anger. He bared his sharp teeth and bit through the knots around the blanket. He pulled the blanket wide and growled. These weren't legs! They were pants stuffed with bags of rice.

"What is the meaning of this?" Grissel yelled. "We've been tricked!"

The Goblins jumped onto the floor beside the trunk and pulled the rope away from the rest of the blanket. They couldn't have been tricked. Not by a human child!

"Aha!" a voice yelled behind them. They turned just in time to be splashed in the face with a bucket of icy water.

The Goblins yelped and screamed and fell backward into the trunk. All except for Grissel, who had escaped the worst of the water by hiding behind the other Goblins. He poofed back to Flog with only three water welts on his arm.

Elliot darted forward and slammed the lid to his trunk closed, locked it, and then sat on it. This was very difficult to do, because the Goblins were beating against the inside of it very angrily. More than once, they nearly tipped Elliot and his trunk sideways onto the floor.

"Quiet down in there, Elliot," his father called from the bedroom down the hall. "You should be sleeping, not playing."

"Sorry," Elliot called back, although none of the playing

he'd ever done before involved real Goblins trying to stuff him in a trunk.

The trunk rumbled again. "Are you sure they're stuck in there?" Elliot asked Mr. Willimaker, who had just tiptoed out from his hiding place in the closet.

"You're a king in the Underworld," Mr. Willimaker said. "Command them to stay in there and they must, until you release them."

Elliot's eyes widened. "I just say 'stay in the trunk' and they have to do it?"

Mr. Willimaker shrugged. "You could wave your arm around so it looks fancy, but only if you want to. It doesn't really matter, because as long as you say the words, they have to obey."

"Can I command them to do anything I want?"

"Not with Brownie magic. Possibly you can command them to sing your favorite song in three-part harmony. But unless you want your ears to shatter, I'd recommend against it. All you can do is command them to remain as your prisoners and not poof away. Since you rule in the Underworld, they're bound by your command to stay."

"It's still pretty cool." Elliot waved his arms the way he'd seen a wizard in a movie do it once, then said, "Hey, you Goblins in the trunk. Stay in there."

The pounding got louder, but the trunk stopped banging

around as much. "I don't think they liked my command," Elliot said.

"They'll give up after a while and go to sleep," Mr. Willimaker said. "They'll be fine until we figure out what to do with them."

"Was that magic?" Elliot asked. "Can I do magic now?"

"I don't know." Mr. Willimaker stretched out his arms then flicked his fingers apart. In his palm was a small puff of smoke that swirled in the air and disappeared. "Can you do that?"

Elliot stretched his arms and flicked his fingers apart. Mr. Willimaker looked at his palms and said, "Oh, my!"

"What do you see?" Elliot asked.

"Dirty hands. You should've used some of the water you threw on the Goblins for yourself."

Elliot looked at his hands and then shoved them in his pockets.

"You don't have magic," Mr. Willimaker said. "But as long as you are king, your command for a prisoner to remain where he is must be obeyed."

Elliot thought of his younger twin brothers. "I wish I could make Kyle and Cole obey my commands."

Mr. Willimaker coughed. "That'd take a miracle, not magic."

"Very impressive," Fudd Fartwick said, coming forward from the shadows. "I must say the Goblins were no match for you, Your Highness." He raised his voice loudly enough so the Goblins inside the trunk could hear him. "It appears the Goblins didn't realize that Mr. Willimaker would tell you about the water. They should've planned something more foolproof." He turned to Mr. Willimaker. "Go poof somewhere and get King Elliot a glass of water. I'm sure he's thirsty."

Elliot wasn't. Half his room was soaked in water. But Mr. Willimaker was gone before he had a chance to say so. However, he quickly understood that Fudd was only trying to get Mr. Willimaker out of the room.

"Be careful of taking any advice from Mr. Willimaker," Fudd warned. "In Burrowsville he's nothing more than a joke. Not a joke as in, 'Why did the giant cross the road? His foot was already on the other side.' But still a joke."

"Queen Bipsy trusted him enough to give him my name as king."

"Only because nobody else was around at the time. Trust *me* instead. I'll keep you safe."

Elliot nodded. "Thank you, Fudd. I'm sure I'll need your help too. But Mr. Willimaker has given me good advice so far. I don't care what the rest of Burrowsville thinks of him. He's my friend."

"Thank you, Your Highness." Mr. Willimaker stood behind Elliot with a glass of water in his hands. He lowered his eyes and said, "I am a joke in Burrowsville, that's true. I made a big mistake about a field mouse invasion a few years ago, but I've learned a lot since then. If you want me to leave—"

"The Goblins would've gotten me tonight if it hadn't been for you," Elliot said. "No, Mr. Willimaker, I don't want you to leave."

Mr. Willimaker's ears perked up. "Whether they laugh at me in Burrowsville or not, I'll still serve you the best I can."

"Your best isn't good enough for Elliot," Fudd said. He threw up his hands and kicked at the trunk, which bounced again on the floor. Then he looked at Elliot. "So you threw water on a few Goblins. Do you think that makes you prepared to be a king? Do you think you could fight off somebody like Kovol?"

The air in the room seemed to change when Fudd said that name, as if a cold wind of warning was blowing through. Then Elliot looked at the wafting curtains over Reed's bed and shrugged. "Oh, the window's open." He shut it and asked, "Who's Kovol?"

Mr. Willimaker's eyes darted from side to side, and his voice shook when he spoke. "I'm sure Kovol is nothing to worry about, nothing at all. As long as he stays asleep, which I'm sure he will for another thousand years, then we're fine."

Kovol wouldn't sleep for another night if the Brownies visited him as often as they visited Elliot's house, Elliot thought with a yawn.

"Never mind about Kovol," Fudd said. "You have enough trouble with the Goblins. Mr. Willimaker helped you tonight and you got lucky. I don't think you'll be so lucky next time."

"Next time?" Elliot said.

"Oh, yes." Fudd's thin eyes widened until Elliot could almost see what color they were. Almost. "There will be a next time. And the next time will be far worse."

Mr. Willimaker rubbed his hands together nervously. "In the meantime, Your Highness, perhaps I could have the Brownies help out downstairs. There's a squeak on your staircase we could fix. Or how about a delicious breakfast of fried eggs?"

"No, thanks," Elliot mumbled, moving from the trunk to his bed. "I'm not hungry anymore." His trunk full of Goblins rattled again, reminding Elliot that, yes, they would be back. And, no, it wouldn't be so easy the next time.

Chapter 12

Where Patches Finds the Best Hiding Place Ever

DOWN IN HER HOLE, PATCHES WAS GETTING HUNGRY FOR another carrot. Happily, she didn't have long to wait before another one was lowered to her on a rope, again held just out of her reach. It smelled of turnip juice, and Patches's mouth watered.

Like me, Dear Reader, I'm sure your mouth began watering for some turnip juice when you read that. You should stop reading this book and get yourself some turnip juice right now. If someone in your family just drank the last cupful, then don't be sad. You can make your own.

To make turnip juice, get the biggest pot in your kitchen and fill it with fresh turnips. If you wish to add any of your other favorite vegetables, such as asparagus or Brussels sprouts, that's fine too. Boil until they're tender, and then dump them out on your kitchen floor. Smash the soft turnips with your feet, and gather up any juice that squishes between your toes. It's a treat your whole family will enjoy!

Patches wanted the carrot that had been boiled in turnip juice, but first she was ready to have some fun.

"I don't care what happens to King Elliot anymore," Patches said, trying to sound angry and tired. "Just get rid of him so I can go home."

Actually, she wasn't in too much of a hurry to get home. She had a lot of chores waiting for her there. Cleaning her room was the hardest job, since it was made of dirt and, therefore, was always dirty. Besides, the Goblins made very yummy carrots that she didn't have to share with anyone.

"Tell me how to get rid of the king, then," Grissel said. "The not foolproof plan didn't work."

"I was thinking about chocolate cake. It punishes Brownies, right? So it's certain to punish a human."

"Are you sure?" Grissel asked.

"Last time I was with the humans, I saw a mother put a chocolate cake on the table. She said it was bad for her diet and she shouldn't have any. She finally took some, probably so her children wouldn't have to eat it all. But I heard her say she only wanted a very small piece. It must have been awful for her."

Grissel smugly folded his arms. "Chocolate cake it is. And without the frosting or milk, of course."

"Of course," Patches agreed. "You can call it the Chocolate Cake of Horror."

"Yes," Grissel said. "The Horrifying Chocolate Cake of Horrible Horror."

Patches thought her name was better, but she let it pass.

A short time later, Elliot found a round, double-layer chocolate cake waiting on his doorstep. The Goblins had added extra chocolate to the recipe, just to make his suffering even worse. They also put shaved pieces of chocolate bar on top. When he found it, Elliot showed it to his Uncle Rufus, who happened to have a shiny gold plate under his coat to set it on. Wendy added a few cherries around the outside, and Cole and Kyle even washed their muddy hands before eating it. It made for a beautiful dessert, even without frosting or milk.

Patches was ready the next day for an even better way to trick the Goblins. It was clear that Goblins knew very little about humans, because she could tell them almost anything and they'd try it. As long as she kept this up, King Elliot would be safe. She waited all morning for them to come get her next idea. It had to do with tricking the Goblins into finding some Leprechaun gold to give Elliot. She thought Elliot would like that. But they didn't come. Morning turned to afternoon, and now she really wanted them to come, because she also wanted a carrot.

Patches stared up at the surface. Somewhere up there was a pile of carrots. She could smell them.

Normally, Brownies aren't very good climbers. Their plump bodies are better made for playing on the ground. However, a hungry Brownie is able to do many things a not-so-hungry Brownie wouldn't normally do.

She had to climb the rock wall. And she had to do it now, before anyone came to check on her.

Patches stared up at the rock hole. It was about ten feet to the surface, which is pretty far when you're only two feet tall. There were no branches to hold on to. There was no dirt she could kick at to make a step for her foot.

Patches studied the rock wall. It wasn't smooth and flat. The wall was like a climbing puzzle. Near the bottom was a chunk that stuck out a little. She could fit a toe there. To her right, if she stretched for it, there was a tiny little ledge. She could get a good grip on the rock with her fingers. She really could do this. Or at least she could try.

Patches grabbed some rock and began to climb.

Very slowly and carefully, she found more pieces of the puzzle. There was always another way to move higher. Sometimes it meant moving to the side. Sometimes she had to reach farther than her arm thought it could reach. The effort took all her muscles, some of which she didn't know she had until they began to get tired and almost allowed her to drop off the wall. Patches told her muscles she was sorry for making them work so hard and promised to forget about them once she got home. Her muscles agreed to the deal and continued to help her climb.

Bit by bit, Patches moved closer to the top of the hole.

When she was halfway up, she stole a quick peek below her. She was farther up than she had thought, and the ground looked very far away.

A few Goblins at the top of the rock hole began talking.

Patches froze against the wall. The last thing she needed was to be found out now. The Goblins had kept her alive because they wanted her help in getting King Elliot. But they hadn't come for her help today. Before long, they'd decide that the best help she could give was to sit quietly while they ate her.

The talking at the top of the hole turned to fighting. She couldn't hear everything they said, but she did catch some words like "guard the carrots" and "your turn." It sounded as if one of them had chased the others away from the hole, and pretty soon it was quiet again. Patches continued her tricky climb.

She was so tired by the time she reached the top of the hole that she wanted to curl up and go to sleep right there on the surface. But there was a very good chance that if she did sleep, the next time she woke up it would be inside a Goblin belly. That thought gave her enough energy to crawl behind a pile of rocks and hide.

Patches had never been in Flog before. The city was dark and dirty, and the wind had a smell of rotting fish. No wonder the Goblins were making war against the Brownies. Burrowsville was so beautiful compared to this place. Once the Goblins won the war, they could take over Burrowsville. It wouldn't be long before they ruined it, just as they had ruined Flog. After all, Goblins were the only creatures she knew who had planted their garbage and actually gotten something to grow.

Two voices were coming toward her.

Patches quickly looked around for a better place to hide. These rocks wouldn't keep a Goblin from smelling her. Behind her was a small cave. Her ears tingled. She was sure she *heard* carrots inside. Lots of fat, juicy carrots inviting her to come and hide with them for a while. What polite carrots they were. Such very nice carrots.

Maybe that wasn't actually true. Patches knew she must be very, very hungry if she thought carrots were talking to her. But she had to find somewhere to hide fast and couldn't think of a luckier place. She ran into the cave only seconds before the voices came right up to the rock hole.

"I told you Patches was tricking you," the first voice said. "Humans happen to love chocolate cake!"

Patches's ears perked up. That was Fudd Fartwick's voice! What was Fudd doing in Flog?

"You also told me Patches knows all about humans," the second voice said. "You want to get rid of the human king. I thought maybe Patches did too."

Patches knew that second voice. It belonged to Grissel. If Fudd and Grissel were here together, then Fudd must be helping the Goblins. How could Fudd do such a thing?

Unaware that Patches was hiding only a few feet behind him, Grissel called down into the hole. "Do you hear that, Brownie girl? I'm not using any more of your ideas, and you're not getting any more of our carrots. You're not so smart after all!"

Inside the cave, Patches barely breathed. She was sure the only reason Grissel couldn't smell her in here was because she was surrounded by so many carrots.

"She didn't answer," Grissel said. "Now that's just rude."

But Fudd wasn't interested in Patches's manners at the moment. "I don't know why you have bothered with these simple plans to get King Elliot," he said. "Why not go and scare him to death?"

Grissel sighed as if he were annoyed. "In the first place, scaring someone to death is not as easy as it looks. In the second place, you were the one who said Patches's plans would work. And in the third place, scaring someone to death is not as easy as it looks."

"You already said that one," Fudd said.

Grissel paused and counted on his fingers. "Oh. All right, then, there's only two reasons. So that's what we'll do. The Goblins will scare the human king to death. It's what I wanted in the first place, before Patches talked me out of it."

Fudd clapped his hands together. "This will work. I know it. By tomorrow this will all be over!"

Inside the cave, Patches got ready to run. As soon as Grissel and Fudd left, she had to find a way to warn King Elliot of how much danger he was in.

Fudd and Grissel began to walk away, and then Grissel called to a Goblin who passed by. "Hey, you! Why isn't this carrot cave being guarded? Who's supposed to be here?"

"I dunno," a Goblin with a deep voice answered.

"Then you will stand here and guard these carrots until you can find the Goblin who belongs here!"

"Yes, sir, Grissel. I won't let you down."

Patches sunk onto her pile of carrots. What good was it

to be free of the rock hole if she was now trapped inside this cave? Trapped, and the only one who knew the terrible danger that awaited King Elliot.

Where a Has-Been Hag
Enters the Story

EVEN THOUGH HE WAS NOW KING OF THE BROWNIES, ELLIOT still had to go to school the next day. He was just about to start a spelling test when he suddenly screamed out loud.

"Mr. Penster?" Ms. Blundell, his teacher, stood up from her desk. "Is there a problem?"

As a matter of fact, there was. Elliot had screamed out loud because Mr. Willimaker appeared on his desk. Elliot had nearly written his name and the date on Mr. Willimaker's foot.

"They can't see or hear me," Mr. Willimaker quickly said. "Brownies can be invisible when we need to be. But only for a short time, because it uses a lot of magic. Besides, invisibility makes my head tingle, so it would be helpful if we could talk in private."

"Elliot?" Ms. Blundell prompted.

"There's no problem." Elliot had to tilt his head around Mr. Willimaker to see his teacher's face.

"Are you okay?" Ms. Blundell asked.

"But there is a problem, Your Highness," Mr. Willimaker said.

"Hush," Elliot whispered, but not quietly enough.

Ms. Blundell folded her arms and walked down the aisle, where she stopped at Elliot's desk. "What did you say to me?"

"Er, I meant hush-choo!" Elliot faked a sneeze as he said it. A few kids in class laughed. Ms. Blundell wasn't amused. Harold, the class hamster, wasn't amused either. But, then, nobody expected Harold to be amused. After all, hamsters are known for running on wheels, not for their sense of humor.

Ms. Blundell gave Elliot a warning glance and then walked back to the head of the class. "The first word on your test is 'secret,'" she said. "As in, 'Someone in our class has a really big secret.'"

Elliot looked around. Did anyone suspect he had a secret? "Move," he mumbled as quietly as he could to Mr. Willimaker. "I can't see the teacher."

"Too bad," an annoying, toad-faced girl sitting in front of Elliot said. "I'm not going anywhere."

Elliot rolled his eyes and then stared at Mr. Willimaker. If he wanted something, he'd better say it, because Elliot wasn't going to speak another word.

Mr. Willimaker did have something to say. "Your Highness, you have some official business to attend to."

Elliot shook his head.

"I know that you're in class, but this is very important. We've had a stray wander into Burrowsville. She won't leave, and she's upsetting the Brownies."

"I'm taking a test," he whispered.

"Yes, Mr. Penster, we know," Ms. Blundell snapped. "Now be quiet. The second word on the test is 'annoying,' as in, 'Someone in this class is being annoying.'"

"She said she'll only talk to our king," Mr. Willimaker said.

Elliot huffed. Whoever *she* was, her problem had better be important. He raised his hand and asked, "Can I please go to the bathroom, Ms. Blundell?"

"Can't this wait until the end of the test?"

Elliot glared at Mr. Willimaker. "I guess not."

"You can't make this test up later. If you use the bathroom now, you'll get a zero on the test."

"I've really got to go," Elliot said. The class laughed again, even though he wasn't trying to be funny.

Ms. Blundell pursed her lips. "Then you'll get a zero," she said. "You need to be back in two minutes."

Twelve seconds later, Elliot was in the hall with Mr. Willimaker, running along beside him to keep up. Mr.

Willimaker ran so fast that he kept tripping over his own feet, but Elliot didn't slow down. He wanted to get this over with. He had only two minutes, after all.

"I thought we could all talk in the boys' bathroom," Mr. Willimaker huffed, already out of breath from running.

"You brought a girl into the boys' bathroom?"

"Better than making you go into the girls' bathroom."

That was true. Few things could ruin a boy's entire life faster than being caught in a girls' bathroom. He pushed open the door to the boys' bathroom. Luckily, it was empty.

Or was it?

It sounded as if someone was crying in one of the stalls. Specifically, the disabled stall. He glanced at Mr. Willimaker, who nodded that, yes, this was the person whom Elliot had come to see. Great. Not only a girl in the boys' bathroom, but a crying one.

"Hello?" Elliot walked toward the stall. "Are you okay—wah!"

The crying had been so gentle, he had expected to see someone more, well…gentle. He froze, knowing it was rude to look but too horrified to turn away.

The woman in the stall looked a little like Dorcas, the really mean school lunch lady—but only *if* Dorcas had been turned into a zombie, and only *if* Dorcas wanted to serve children for lunch instead of the mystery meat they usually served. Except this woman was way less cool than zombies and, if possible, even uglier.

She was a woman whose face looked like one of those shriveled apple heads. If you could count the age of a tree by its rings, then maybe you could count her age by her wrinkles. If so, then she was at least seven hundred years old. She had wrinkles on top of her wrinkles. Her tattered clothes were wrinkled. Even her white hair was wrinkled.

"Her name is Agatha, Your Highness," Mr. Willimaker said. "Agatha, this is King Elliot."

"Stare if you must," Agatha said, wiping her tears with a fistful of toilet paper. "Few people can turn away from my beauty."

Elliot giggled and then stopped himself by clasping a hand over his mouth. He didn't mean to be rude, but that wasn't what he expected her to say. Beauty was definitely not the word running through his mind.

Her withered skin looked as if it were made of dry oatmeal. Her face had no less than a dozen warts. Her right eye bulged out from her head so far, he wondered why it didn't fall out. Her hands reminded him of the display skeleton in Ms. Blundell's classroom. Her fingers looked twelve inches long.

"What?" she asked. "You don't think I'm beautiful?"

Elliot remembered the rhyme his first-grade class had said every day at the end of school: "I am beautiful because I'm me. I'll be the best that I can be."

He said, "I believe you are the best you can be."

It was the wrong thing to say.

Dear Boy Readers: When any girl asks you if she's beautiful, it's always a good idea to insist quickly that yes, she is, no matter what she looks like. Even if she has worms in her hair and only one tooth (that for some reason is polka-dotted), you should still find something nice to say about her. If you tell her that she is not pretty, then I hope your family has a bomb shelter in your backyard where you can live for several years, because that will be the only safe place you can hide from her and all of her friends.

Agatha pointed a finger at Elliot. "I happen to be the most beautiful woman in all of everywhere. Since you can't see that, I've decided to curse you."

Elliot took a step back. "That's not very nice. Did you know I got a zero on my spelling test just to come help you?"

"Quiet," she hissed. "It's hard to curse you when you're talking. Here is the curse: I am a hag. My beauty is plain. Because you can't see it. You'll soon feel a brain."

Elliot blinked. "Eww. What brain?"

"I think she meant you'll soon feel pain, Your Highness," Mr. Willimaker said. "One moment, Agatha." Mr. Willimaker shut the door to the toilet stall and then pulled Elliot several steps away.

"What's a hag?" Elliot asked. "Why is she here?"

Mr. Willimaker shook his head. "Actually, she's a has-been hag. As you can tell from her curse, she's sort of lost her touch."

"What does this have to do with me?"

"She came to Burrowsville last night looking for a place to stay until she figures out how to get her cursing powers back. She keeps cursing all the Brownies, and it's starting to upset them."

Elliot couldn't believe what he was hearing. He'd agreed to get a zero on a spelling test because of a has-been hag who'd lost her powers of cursing? "Can't you just send her away?" he asked.

Mr. Willimaker bit his lip. "I had this idea, Your Highness. It's probably a terrible one, because my ideas usually aren't very good, but I thought maybe she could help us win the Goblin war."

"How?" Elliot demanded.

"What if she does get her cursing powers back?" Mr. Willimaker asked.

Elliot grinned. "And then she curses the Goblins?"

Mr. Willimaker nodded. "Exactly. But we have to find a place for her to stay in the meantime."

Elliot opened the bathroom stall again and held out a hand for her to shake. "We started out badly, Agatha. My name is Elliot."

She took his hand and shook it and then quickly pulled his hand to her mouth and bit his finger.

"Ow!" Elliot pulled his hand away. "What was that for?"

"I cursed you to feel pain," Agatha said. "Look, it already happened."

Elliot almost smiled. "Only because you bit me. If you make it happen, then it's not a real curse."

"It was a real pain, though." Then tears formed in Agatha's eyes. "Oh, you're right. What kind of a hag am I if I can't even curse a human child?"

"I'm sure you're a very good hag. Maybe you're just tired." Elliot rubbed his bit finger but stopped as he heard a voice in the hallway. Someone was coming into the bathroom. He shoved Mr. Willimaker into Agatha's stall and hissed, "Keep her quiet!"

He slammed the stall door closed.

Tubs! Of course, it had to be Tubs who came in.

Tubs's eyes narrowed. "What are you doing in here, Penster? I told you this was my bathroom."

Elliot shrugged. "I checked for your name on the bathroom door. It said 'boys' bathroom.' Since your name isn't 'boys,' I thought it'd be okay."

Tubs ran that idea through his mind. About halfway through it got lost in empty space, so Tubs let it drop.

"Move," Tubs said. "I want to use that stall."

Elliot kept his back firmly against the stall door. "It's for people who need it. Use a different one."

"I don't want a different one. I like a stall with a lot of space."

Elliot's legs shook, but he held his ground. Behind him, he thought he heard Agatha sniffle.

"What was that?" Tubs asked. "Are you hiding someone in there?"

Elliot smiled. "Like who? A beautiful young woman disguised as a hag who's just waiting to curse you?"

Tubs paused. "Uh, maybe. Now move!"

"You can't have this stall, Tubs."

Tubs darted to Elliot and grabbed his arms, lifting Elliot off the ground. "Ever been flushed down a toilet, Penster?"

Elliot never had. And it didn't sound fun. He kicked and squirmed, but Tubs kept a tight hold on him as he carried Elliot to the other stall.

"What the—" Tubs said.

Elliot looked down. Tubs's pants had fallen down around his ankles. Tubs set Elliot down and pulled his pants up again. They fell again, almost as if someone yanked them down. His underwear had little red hearts on it. Elliot had to bite his tongue hard to keep from giggling. Tubs pulled his pants up, this time keeping his hands on them to hold them in place.

"Tell you what," Tubs said. "If you don't tell anyone about my pants, I won't tell them you're hiding someone in here."

"Deal." Elliot nearly laughed as Tubs ran out of the

bathroom. He opened the stall and smiled down at Mr. Willimaker. "Thanks for that."

Mr. Willimaker bowed his head. "My pleasure. Now, what shall we do with Agatha?"

Elliot scratched his chin. "Why don't you come home with me for a few days, Agatha? I'm sure my parents will let you stay, and you can keep my Uncle Rufus company."

Agatha stood. "Okay, but I still may have to curse you again."

That didn't matter to Elliot. The way he figured, ever since he met the Brownies, he'd already been cursed.

Chapter
14

Where the Reader Is Warned

DEAR READER: MAY I SUGGEST THAT BEFORE YOU BECOME too interested in whether Elliot survives the next Goblin attack, that you close this book now. Remember that chapter 15 is coming up next, and that is the very chapter in which several readers lost valuable body parts. It probably won't happen to you, but it might, and many readers who went on to read chapter 15 later regretted it.

Take the example of Libby Frackenflower, a very smart and

talented fifth grader who was the captain of her baseball team. She didn't heed this warning. Having decided that if she could outlast the meanest teacher in fourth grade, Mrs. Pinchey, then she could certainly survive a chapter of this book.

Sadly, both of Libby's arms fell off about three paragraphs before the end of chapter 15. Now, do not worry for Libby Frackenflower. She has become very good at swinging a baseball bat with her teeth and catching the ball with her belly button, but we feel certain that if she could go back and un-read chapter 15, she would.

You may be laughing at Libby, which isn't polite. But if you can't help it, then please don't laugh while drinking hot cocoa, or else you might giggle the marshmallows right out of your nose.

Dear Reader, please stop now. Because the start of chapter 15 is going to be so good that you'll find you've reached the end before you know it. And for some of you, it will be too late.

Chapter 15

Where Elliot Gets a Lot Scared

THE GOOD NEWS WAS THAT ELLIOT'S FAMILY HAD WARMLY welcomed Agatha the hag into their home. (If you want to call her Hagatha, that's fine. Elliot already thought of it too, even though he didn't dare say it. Don't call her Nagatha or Ragatha, though—no matter how grumpy she is or what her clothes look like—because that's just rude. You can also call her Betsy, but don't expect her to answer, because that's not her name.)

Elliot introduced her as honestly as he could. He told his family that she was a lost woman he met in town who just needed somewhere to stay for a few days.

"She has nothing," Elliot told his parents. "I just feel like we need to help her."

Elliot's father put his arm around Elliot's shoulder. "I

agree. We have almost nothing, and that's way better than plain old nothing. So, yes, we have to help her."

"We always have room for one more," Elliot's mother said. "She can stay in Wendy's room."

Wendy's eyes had widened in fear, and a little vein popped out in her forehead, but she wisely said nothing. Elliot hoped her silence would spare her from being cursed. It didn't.

Cursing was the bad news. Reed had dropped his peanut-butter-and-pickle-relish sandwich when she first entered the kitchen, mumbling something about the walking dead. Agatha pointed a spindly finger at Reed and said, "I am a hag. These looks are for show. I curse you with pain when you stuff a crow."

"What was that?" Reed asked. "You want me to stuff a crow?"

"I think she means 'stub a toe,'" Elliot said. "Right, Agatha?"

Reed nodded, a bit confused. "Oh, okay. I didn't know where I was going to find a crow." As he walked past Agatha, she suddenly raised a leg up and then stomped on Reed's foot.

"Ow!" Reed yelped. "What was that for?"

"The curse said you'd stub a toe," Agatha said. "Look, you have."

"You just mashed my toe," Reed said. "That's different! And it hurt!"

"Then you'd better not let yourself get cursed again."

Agatha cursed Wendy as well, telling her she'd soon be

quacked on a farm. Then she whacked Wendy on the arm. Agatha cursed the twins that they'd strut past a bear, but they were smart enough to run away before she could cut their hair. Elliot was pretty sure he heard Agatha also whisper a curse against his parents, although he wasn't sure what it was. When his father limped past Elliot that afternoon, he said, "Next time, I get to choose our house guest."

But Agatha poured most of her energy into keeping Elliot fully stocked with fresh curses. By dinnertime, Elliot had already been cursed four times. He stopped paying attention to most of her rhymes. She didn't have any actual cursing power and was only finding a reason to cause everyone a little pain. He'd learned to avoid most of Tubs's hits. He could avoid hers too.

The fifth curse came shortly after dinner when Elliot took his plate to the sink but forgot to take hers. She pointed at him and said, "I am a hag and this curse is your own. The Goblin leader you must face alone."

Hoping she hadn't just exposed his secret, Elliot quickly looked around, but he and Agatha were alone in the room. Then he began to worry. For the first time since he met Agatha, she had used the right word in her cursing rhymes. And facing the Goblin leader alone sounded pretty bad to him.

Fudd knew the Goblins better than anyone. He had spent a lot of time warning Elliot about what terrible things they might try next. Whoever was mean enough to lead the Goblins was someone Elliot preferred to avoid.

But he didn't think he could avoid it now. Agatha had cursed him, and probably with a real curse too.

Or could she be wrong? Maybe another word was supposed to go in there. Maybe she meant, I am a hag and this curse is your own. The Goblin leader you must call on the phone. Or, The Goblin leader, you must give him a loan? Throw him a bone?

Elliot couldn't even smile. Those ideas sounded good, but he was pretty sure he was doomed.

Uncle Rufus was the only family member who hadn't been cursed so far. He'd been gone when Elliot brought the hag home from school. He had also missed dinner.

But when Rufus walked into the house that night, Agatha was the first thing he saw. He put his hands to his heart, his mouth dropped open, and he shook his head as if he couldn't believe what he was seeing.

"Elliot," he whispered, staring at Agatha as if she were more delicious than a double-decker hot fudge sundae. "Where did you find this angel?"

"Huh?" Elliot said.

Agatha glared at Elliot, probably trying to think of another curse.

"Go on, kind sir," Agatha said with a giggle. In anyone else's voice, her words would have sounded sweet. Coming from Agatha's mouth, the words sounded as if they came from a toad choking on a mushroom.

"I have lived many years all over this world," Uncle Rufus said. "I've seen majestic waterfalls tumbling into glistening lakes. I've seen sunsets that have made me weep. I've seen endless wildflower meadows and laid down in them to count the clouds. But you, my lady, are the most beautiful thing I have ever set eyes upon."

Elliot shook his head. Either Uncle Rufus had gone blind or else he was smarter than the rest of his family at not getting himself cursed.

Uncle Rufus nudged Elliot on the shoulder. "Be a good little girl and get me some of those earrings I gave you last year."

"I'm a boy, Uncle Rufus," Elliot muttered.

"And a fine boy you are. Now go get me some of your earrings. I can't introduce myself to this beautiful woman without a gift to offer her."

Elliot ran to get the earrings, but a gift wasn't necessary. When he got back downstairs, Rufus and Agatha were already sitting on the couch together, laughing as if they were old friends.

He set the earrings on the table and walked outside to sit on his front porch. Maybe Agatha really was a beautiful young woman. Maybe that was part of what it meant to be a hag. If so, why could Uncle Rufus see who she really was, but none of the rest of his family could?

"Psst, look over here," a voice whispered.

(You, the reader, have learned exactly what it means when something whispers, "Psst, look over here." However, Elliot has not read this book, so he doesn't know exactly how Queen Bipsy died.)

Elliot peered into the shadows of his yard, not sure where the *here* was where he was supposed to look.

"Psst, this way," the voice whispered again.

Elliot walked off his porch. To his right was a little clump of bushes. Very slowly, something crawled from them. Elliot's memory flashed to when he was eight years old, facing what he thought were kids dressed in Halloween costumes, but who were actually Goblins. Whatever had happened then was happening again.

Only there were five of them this time.

Five Goblins with boiling, bubbling skin. With each bubble, they grew larger and blacker. Their skin was wet, and in the moonlight Elliot saw bulges form along their back and down their arms and legs.

Run! Elliot's brain screamed it to him, but not loudly enough to get his legs to listen. He could do nothing but stare at the emerging beasts.

His heart beat faster, pounding against the wall of his chest. Pounding in rhythm with the bubbling skin.

The Goblins' faces were changing too. Their jagged teeth,

already protruding from their wide mouths, grew into a mouthful of fangs. The ends of their fingers extended into claws long enough to pry a door off its hinges, and their coloring darkened to a sooty dark green. The Goblins banged their teeth together, and the earth shook beneath Elliot's feet. The yard swirled around him. Everything was in a dizzy motion except for the monsters before him. He could see them all too well.

Elliot's breath locked in his throat, and he gasped for air. His lungs must have shut down, because they didn't want to help him breathe anymore. They only wanted to get away from this. His heart knocked unevenly now, like it couldn't keep up with the rhythm from the Goblins' gnashing teeth.

Elliot's eyes rolled back in his head, and he fell to the ground. Someone ran into the yard with a broom. Was it Agatha? She moved fast for a woman her age. She swung the broom at the monsters, and they clawed back at her. She started yelling at them, although he couldn't hear the words...just the pounding rhythm.

It was the rhythm that mattered.

The rhymes. Agatha's curses were in rhyme.

Suddenly, the air filled with light and all went silent. Elliot closed his eyes, and just as quickly, his world went black.

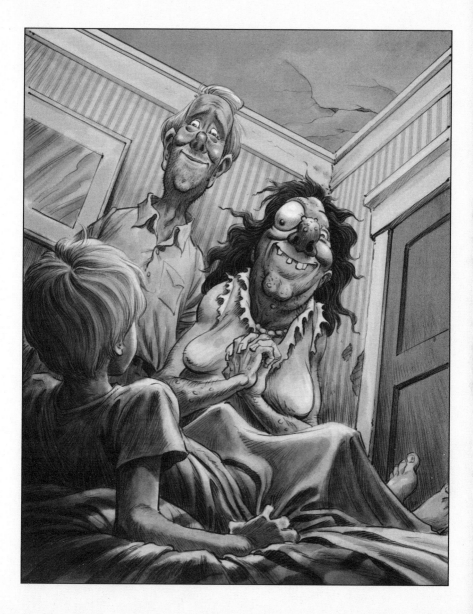

Chapter 16

Where Elliot Might Be a Zombie

THE FIRST THING ELLIOT HEARD WAS GIGGLING. HE DIDN'T expect to hear giggling, because surely he had been scared to death by the Goblins, and whoever thought that being scared to death was funny was just plain rude.

Tubs was rude, and Tubs also might have thought Elliot's death was funny, but Tubs never giggled. So who was it?

Elliot opened one eye, just a peek to see who might be giggling, but he couldn't see anyone. Then he thought maybe he wasn't dead after all. Because if there's one thing dead people can't do, it's open their eyes to peek at the living world.

Elliot did an official test to see if he was alive. He wiggled his toes.

Uncle Rufus once told him a story about a dead person who wiggled their toes. It had something to do with the body's nerves still working for a few hours after death. Elliot gasped. Maybe he was one of those stories! Now all he had to do was figure out how to become a zombie. How cool was that?

Then his brain woke up and told him to stop dreaming. If he was going to become a zombie, then he'd be out on the streets moaning already. Not lying in a bed listening to someone giggle. He was definitely alive, and it was time to wake up.

Uncle Rufus and Agatha stared down at him. Agatha's bulging left eye looked as if it were ready to fall out at any second. Elliot shifted in his bed so it wouldn't land on him, just in case.

"Quiet now," Agatha said. "Don't get up too fast."

"You saved me from those—" Elliot stopped and looked at Uncle Rufus. He knew he couldn't say anything about the Brownies. That probably meant he couldn't talk about the Goblins either.

"He knows," Agatha said.

Elliot sat up on his elbows. "He knows what?"

"I know about Agatha," Uncle Rufus said, smiling. "It wasn't hard to figure out once I realized everyone saw something different than I did."

"Why can you see her and nobody else can?" Elliot asked.

"You'll see her too, in time," Uncle Rufus said.

"Oh." Elliot stole a hopeful glance at Agatha, just in case. It didn't work. She was still the most hideous creature he'd ever seen. He looked back to Uncle Rufus. "Where's my family?"

"Off to work or school, so it's just us to take care of you," he said.

Agatha tapped Uncle Rufus on the arm. "Elliot will be thirsty, dear," she hissed. "Will you get him a drink of water?"

Dear? Just how long had Elliot been asleep?

As soon as Uncle Rufus left, Agatha turned to him. "Your uncle knows about me, but that's all. He thinks the Goblins came to find me and knows nothing about the Brownies. Your secret is safe."

"Can we tell him?"

Agatha shook her head. "If he figures it out, then that's one thing. But the secrets of the Underworld don't belong to you. You can keep their secrets, but it's not your right to tell them."

Elliot lay back on his bed. "Why did you save me from the Goblins? Ever since I met you, all you've done is curse me."

"Yes, and you're still cursed." Agatha stood and brushed her hands together. "But I didn't curse you to die by being scared to death, now, did I? What kind of hag would I be if you died before I'd finished cursing you?"

"Oh," Elliot said. So maybe the fact that Agatha had saved him wasn't such good news after all. "But your curse came true. You told me I'd face the leader of the Goblins, and I think he was there last night."

Agatha shook her finger at him. "You're not getting out of the curse that easily, young man. I didn't curse you to lose—and trust me, you were losing very badly. I cursed you so that you'd face your fears and win."

"Looks like my fears are going to face me, whether I want them to or not." Elliot took a deep breath and then asked, "Do the Brownies know what happened?"

"Yes. Mr. Willimaker has been here several times since last night. He's very worried about you. Fudd visited you too. He didn't stay long, just checked your heartbeat and banged his head on the wall. I'm sure Mr. Willimaker will visit again soon."

"I'm sure he will." Elliot had seen more of Mr. Willimaker lately than his own family. "So that's what it's like, being scared to death, huh?"

"You were only *mostly* scared to death. Trust me, there's a big difference. But the Goblins will be tired after that big show. You're probably safe for the rest of the day."

Probably safe. That also didn't sound like good news. Elliot chewed his lip and then asked, "Agatha, is there someone in the Underworld named Kovol? Fudd said something about him, that he's asleep."

Almost all of the color drained from Agatha's face. All of

the color but a strange shade of yellow, which was very unsettling. Elliot was relieved when the color returned and she said, "Kovol. Why would a nice boy like you want to know about him?"

"I just want to know. He's pretty evil, right?"

Agatha frowned. "He's a demon, not a kitty cat. Of course he's evil."

Elliot leaned up on his elbows. "Is he someone so scary that nobody even dares to say his name aloud?"

"Are you kidding? We say his name all the time!" Agatha chuckled. Then her face darkened and she added, "But seriously, though, he is scary. He's the last of the Underworld demons. He's been asleep for the past thousand years, and the last I heard, he was still sleeping peacefully. You don't have to worry about him, Elliot. Just worry about the Goblins. They're trouble enough for one human boy."

Uncle Rufus returned with the water and handed it to Elliot. At about the same time, Mr. Willimaker appeared at the foot of Elliot's bed, scaring Elliot so much he jumped and spilled water all over the room.

"I'll...uh, get you another glass," Uncle Rufus muttered. Obviously, he couldn't see Mr. Willimaker. "This time I'll bring one with a lid."

Agatha winked at Elliot as she followed Rufus out of the room. He wondered if she winked because she could see Mr.

Willimaker, or if she were closing her eye to keep her bulging eyeball from falling out of her head.

Elliot turned to Mr. Willimaker, who bowed so low his nose nearly touched the blankets. "Your Highness, I can't believe what happened. Had I known—"

"Had you known, then what?" Elliot interrupted. "Could you have protected me from the Goblins?"

Mr. Willimaker shook his head. "Well, no, I'm afraid not. The Goblins are much stronger than us Brownies. It seems they are stronger than you too."

Elliot stubbornly folded his arms. "No, they're not. I just wasn't ready for them last night. Now I am, and that'll never work on me again."

Mr. Willimaker smiled and sat on Elliot's bed. "I believe you, Your Highness, and admire your bravery. What are your plans now?"

"I dunno. Get better and hope they don't try to kill me again before I go back to school tomorrow? My Uncle Rufus takes good care of Agatha, so I don't have to worry about her being here."

Mr. Willimaker smiled. "Yes, I saw Agatha when I poofed in here. She seems happier."

"She saved me from the Goblins. I think she's going to get her cursing powers back. When that happens, we'll find a way for her to curse them once and for all."

"What if she doesn't?" Mr. Willimaker asked.

Elliot hadn't thought about that. "This war has to end before the Goblins get me," he said. "Better start thinking, Mr. Willimaker, because if Agatha doesn't get her cursing powers back, it'll be up to you and me to solve this problem."

Mr. Willimaker swallowed a lump in his throat. If Elliot needed his help to solve this problem, then they were definitely in trouble.

Where Fudd Needs Pixie Magic

PATCHES HAD DECIDED THERE WERE WORSE THINGS THAN being stuck in the cave full of carrots. It was better here than at school, where all the other Brownie kids still teased her about her father and the field mouse scare. It was better than being stuck in the rock hole, where she had only gotten a single carrot after she told them an idea to get King Elliot. However, it was *not* better than going on vacation to Underworld World, the happiest place under the earth. But that was an entirely different matter.

For now, all Patches cared about was being stuck. Every time she tried to sneak out, the Goblin guarding the cave peeked inside as if he'd heard—or smelled—her. Trapped with nothing to do but eat carrots left Patches with more than enough time to think about what might have happened to King Elliot. She'd barely slept all night, so anxious for him that she'd only managed to eat 214 carrots.

It was with great worry the next morning that Patches heard Fudd and Grissel return to the rock hole. Their voices were angry. Patches felt a little relief. If they were arguing, then things had probably not gone the way they wanted with Elliot.

The guard quickly ran off when Grissel ordered him to go away. Then Fudd and Grissel began talking right outside the entrance to the carrot cave.

"Your plan to scare King Elliot to death failed!" Fudd said. "How could it fail? You told me you'd use your scariest Goblins!"

Grissel growled. "I did. They were so good they almost scared *me* to death."

"Then what went wrong?"

"It seems your king has a hag. Her beauty forced us away." Grissel threw out his chunky hands. "Why didn't you tell me Elliot had a hag?"

Fudd sounded offended. "They told me that the hag was broken. I didn't think it was important."

"Well, she wasn't broken last night. Maybe her curses don't work as well as usual, but when she transforms, she puts off a lot of light. She burned my eyes!"

"Ouch. That's why they're so red."

Grissel whimpered. "No, that's because after I came back

I tried to put some burn cream on them. I guess you can't put the cream right on your eye."

Fudd huffed. Even a river troll knew that. "So what now?" he demanded.

"We're done," Grissel said. "Let the Brownies have a human king if they want. We'll continue our war against the Brownies as we have for the last three years. Pretty soon we'll have eaten every Brownie, and there won't be anyone left for the human boy, Elliot Penster, to rule."

"No!" Fudd said, stamping a foot. "The idea is for you to get revenge against Elliot and for me to become the Brownie king! We had an agreement."

"Whatever happens next, you'll have to do it on your own," Grissel said. "So far we've done all the work. If you want to get Elliot, then it's up to you."

Fudd kicked at a rock. It rolled into the cave, not far from where Patches was carefully listening to every word.

So the Goblin plan hadn't worked! Elliot was alive! For now.

"You tried the *not* foolproof plan, and it failed," Fudd mumbled. "You tried the Chocolate Cake of Horror plan, and it failed. Then last night you tried the foolproof plan, and it also failed. So maybe it's time to try something that isn't either one. Something no one can protect Elliot from, because it's never been done before."

"I like it," Grissel said. "Better yet, I love it. Whatever *it* is, it's got to be great!"

"That's right," Fudd agreed. "If it's never been done, then it's never failed yet. And something that has never failed is certain to succeed! We'll do something final. Something really, really awful." Fudd thought about all the plans he'd formed that first night in Elliot's room. Then he smiled. The last idea was so crazy that it just might work. It was evil, cruel, and only required a bit of black market Pixie magic. Besides, rule number twelve in the *Guidebook to Evil Plans* clearly stated, "Think big. Small plans have never produced great villains (page 33)."

Fudd turned to Grissel, his grin so wide it showed most of his pointy teeth. "Wait until tomorrow," he said. "After tomorrow, Elliot Penster, king of the Brownies, will be no more."

Inside the cave, Patches gasped. They were going to get Elliot this time. And there was nothing she could do about it. She had to make a run for it. Her short Brownie legs weren't made for running really fast, but the Goblins didn't know she had escaped the hole. Hopefully they'd be so surprised that she'd get free before they caught her.

Patches waited until it was quiet outside and then took a deep breath and began running. She ran from the cave as fast as she could—maybe as fast as any Brownie had ever run before. But even a fast-running Brownie is still pretty slow. It was no trouble at all for Grissel to grab on to her hair as she exited the cave and pull her back to him.

"Did you think I couldn't smell you in there?" he snarled at her. "Where were you going in such a hurry?"

"I had to warn King Elliot," she said. "I have to help him."

"You will help him," Grissel said with an evil grin. "You'll help him lose." He tossed Patches to a couple of Goblins waiting nearby. "Tie her up good. I have a feeling we're going to need her help soon."

Chapter 18

Where Reed Misses His Shoelaces

DUE TO BEING ALMOST DEAD, ELLIOT HAD MISSED SCHOOL on Thursday. By late afternoon he was completely alive again. He was so completely alive that the rest of his family decided he must've only had a case of the stomach flu the night before. Wendy baked him another cake to celebrate his getting better. Elliot thought it was chocolate, but it was actually a very burned white cake. He crunched it down anyway. Reed brought him a whole bag of pickle relish from the Quack Shack in case he felt like having any. (He didn't.) And Kyle and Cole flooded the woods behind Elliot's house again. Not really to celebrate Elliot getting better. It's just what they liked to do.

The next day was Friday, and if you remember from chapter 9, Elliot had to stay after school for detention because his teacher thought he'd made a joke during science class. He couldn't explain to his teacher at the time why he had Brownies on his mind. And now he was fairly certain that even if he tried to tell the teacher that he was the king of the Brownies, it would only earn him more detention.

As it turned out, getting detention probably saved Elliot's life, because while he was at school, Fudd used his Pixie magic plan. When Elliot came home later that afternoon, he noticed one very different thing about his house. His room was gone.

It wasn't simply that everything *in* his room had disappeared, although that was true. It was that where he once had four walls, a door, and a window, there was nothing.

Elliot patted on the hallway wall where he used to have a door to enter his room. But it was only solid wall.

He walked outside and stared at the new shape of his

home, which now looked as if it were missing a piece, right where his room had been.

"What's wrong?" Wendy said, walking outside.

Elliot pointed at where his room wasn't. "My room is gone."

"Hmm, you used to have a room there. How strange."

"Strange? Do you think?"

Reed came out to join them. "What are you looking at?"

"Our room is gone," Elliot said. "Look."

"Oh, bummer," Reed said. "I had a new pair of shoelaces in there."

Elliot threw up his hands. "Everything was in there!"

"No need to get so angry," Wendy said. "So what if your room disappeared? Did you ever think about the poor kids in this world who never had their own room at all?"

"It doesn't strike you as odd?" Elliot asked.

"I already said it was strange, didn't I?" Wendy said. "But look at Reed. He lost his shoelaces and he's not complaining."

"I'm complaining a little bit," Reed pointed out. "I really liked those shoelaces."

Wendy and Reed entered the house, fighting about who had to call their parents at work and let them know that there was one less bedroom in the house.

"Consider it good news," Cole said. Elliot jumped. He hadn't realized the twins were behind him.

"What's good about this?" Elliot asked.

129

Kyle shrugged. "We were home when it disappeared. It happened right after you usually get home from school. If you had been in your room when it happened, you would've disappeared too."

"So you saw it?"

Cole shook his head. "I don't know if you can *see* something disappear. It's just that we were in your room looking at that shiny bracelet you had, and then your room started to shake. So we ran out really fast. We shut the door and turned around, and the door was gone."

"Where's Agatha?" Elliot asked. Maybe one of her curses had worked. Could she do that? Did she have that much magic?

"Agatha hasn't been here all day," Cole said. "She said she was tired of cursing our family and wanted to curse some of the other people in town for a while."

Elliot's shoulders slumped. He had hoped this would have been Agatha's doing. Because if it wasn't her, then the Goblins were already trying to kill him again. It was a warm Friday afternoon, the start of what should have been a nice weekend. He'd gotten all of his homework done in detention, and wherever in the universe his room was, he'd already cleaned it this morning...so he was really looking forward to a relaxing weekend.

But as you well know, Dear Reader, nothing ends the

fun of a weekend faster than someone trying to kill you all the time.

"Anyway, you're going to be in trouble when Mom comes home," Kyle yelled to Elliot as he and Cole ran away.

"What for?" Elliot yelled back.

"Remember that time we lost our gloves at school? We were grounded for a week. But you went and lost your whole room!"

As soon as his brothers had left, Elliot turned and shouted, "Mr. Willimaker!"

"No need to be so loud, no need for that," said a voice from the trees in Elliot's backyard. "I'm already here."

Elliot trudged into the trees a little ways. He found Mr. Willimaker sitting on a fallen tree stump, his head in his hands and a wide frown on his face.

"I'm so sorry," Mr. Willimaker said. "This is all my fault."

Elliot pressed his eyebrows together, wondering why Mr. Willimaker might need to apologize. After all, he hadn't scared Elliot half to death or made Elliot's room disappear. Elliot didn't know that Mr. Willimaker was actually thinking about how he had written Elliot's name in as king. Queen Bipsy had been one of Mr. Willimaker's last friends in the entire Brownie kingdom. She had believed in him when no one else did. That's why she trusted him to choose the name of the next king. She would be so disappointed now to see that once again, instead of making things better for the Underworld, he had only made them worse.

The future wasn't looking too rosy for Elliot now either.

"I'm sorry, Your Highness," Mr. Willimaker repeated.

"You didn't do this," Elliot said. "Was it the Goblins?"

"It must have been, but I don't understand how they could've done it on their own. Making an entire room disappear needs Pixie magic. But Goblins can't use other creatures' magic. They can only use their own. So they must've had help."

"Whose?"

Mr. Willimaker sighed. "I wish I knew. I hate to say it, but I fear it might be a Brownie who has done this. We don't have a lot of magic of our own, but we are very good at borrowing it from other creatures. If only we had Patches back. She could help us figure this out."

"Can I help to get her back?" Elliot asked.

"I wish you could come with me to the Underworld. The Pixies could poof you there. But since they just helped the Goblins, I don't think they'd help us."

Elliot nodded. "I don't think I'm allowed to go to the Underworld anyway. My parents don't like me to go to new places by myself."

Mr. Willimaker smiled sadly. "King of the Brownies, and you still need permission from your parents."

"But if my parents knew why I was going to the

Underworld, they'd probably understand," Elliot said. "We can't trust the Pixies to poof me there, but you could do it, right?"

Mr. Willimaker's eyes widened. "No, sir. I wouldn't dare, not even to rescue Patches. My magic isn't strong enough to poof a human anywhere. I'd probably get your feet into the Underworld and your head and maybe a few of your fingers, but I'd lose the rest of your body. It'd be very hard to rescue Patches with only half of your body."

"Oh," Elliot said. His parents might understand if he had to go to the Underworld to rescue Patches. They definitely would not understand his having only half a body. "Then we have to think of a different way to save her."

"We will." Mr. Willimaker cocked his head. "Where is your crown, Your Highness?"

Elliot turned to where Cole and Kyle were now at the side of the house. "Wait one minute."

He ran to his brothers. They had dug a ditch in a circle, filled it with water, and then had put several ants on the dirt island in the middle.

"What are you doing?" Elliot asked.

"We want to see what the ants will do," Cole said. "They want to get off the island but can't swim."

"Oh. Where's the cr—I mean, the bracelet you took from my room? You didn't leave it in there, did you?"

"No," Kyle said. "Cole, you had it last. Where'd you put it?"

"I left it in the kitchen. But next time I looked it wasn't there. It's pretty shiny. Maybe Uncle Rufus got it."

Elliot ran back and knelt beside Mr. Willimaker. "My uncle won't lose it or anything. He'll just carry it around for a while, and then I can get it back later."

Mr. Willimaker's face went green, like the color of canned peas. Not a good color for either peas or Brownies. "Do you know why your room disappeared?"

"Because the Goblins knew it was my room. They hoped I'd be in it."

"A king always wears his crown, and if your crown was in your room, then they thought you were in your room. Wherever your crown is now, when the Goblins try again, they'll think they're attacking you."

Elliot stood. "What will they do to the crown?"

Mr. Willimaker shook his head. "Goblins don't make things disappear. They blow them up."

Elliot began racing toward his house. "I've got to find Uncle Rufus!"

But there was no time. He fell onto the grass as a rush of wind knocked him flat on his back. It was followed by a boom. Then his entire house exploded.

Chapter 19

Where Elliot's Problems Get Worse

IT TOOK A MOMENT BEFORE ELLIOT REALIZED EXACTLY WHAT had happened. He stood on shaking legs and staggered toward what just ten seconds ago had been his home. Now it was rubble, a heap of wood and broken pipes and chunks of furniture. Shreds of paper and fabric still rained from the sky like confetti, and there was an eerie silence, as if even the breeze didn't dare make any sound.

In the center of where the Penster home had stood, the bathtub had somehow survived. On top of it was a mattress that had fallen from the second story.

"No, no," Elliot whispered. He sat on what had once been a toilet and buried his face in his hands. The kitchen must have blown this way. He saw pieces of his mother's dishes, half of a chair, and Reed's large jar with his collection of leftover pickle relish in it. A crack ran down the jar where it had landed, but amazingly it hadn't shattered.

If he could have chosen the two things to have left in this world, it probably wouldn't have been a bathtub and a jar of pickle relish. But his luck seemed to work that way lately.

Then he heard a sound. It was muffled, but someone was speaking nearby. "Hello? Hello?"

It came from the bathtub. Elliot pushed the mattress off the top and then smiled with relief. Uncle Rufus was lying inside it, fully clothed, with the crown between his fingers.

"I didn't realize we had such a lovely view of the sky from the bathroom," Rufus said.

"The house blew up," Elliot told him.

"Oh." Uncle Rufus sat up and glanced at the mess around him. "So it did."

"Didn't you hear the explosion?"

Blushing, Uncle Rufus said, "I, er, passed gas. I thought that was what I heard."

"Our whole house exploded," Elliot said. "It was very loud."

"Yes, but I don't hear so well anymore. I thought it was me. What a relief."

"That our house blew up?"

"No, that I don't have gas. Although if I did, it would be a good thing that we're out here in the open air." Rufus

137

remembered the crown between his fingers. "I think this is yours. I thought you might allow me to give it as a gift to Agatha. It was just so shiny, and I know she'd like it. But I shouldn't have taken it without asking you."

"I wish I could let you have it, but I can't give this up now, even if I wanted to." Elliot took the crown and then helped Rufus out of the bathtub. "I have to find everyone else."

But everyone else found him. Wendy walked across the rubble holding Cole and Kyle by the ears. "Look what you two did," she said to them.

"We didn't blow the house up," Cole protested.

"That's just what someone who *did* blow up a house would say," Wendy replied.

"We promise," Kyle insisted. "Tell them, Elliot. You saw us outside. Did it look like we were blowing up the house?"

"They didn't blow up the house," Elliot told his sister. "Where's Reed? Is he okay?"

Wendy released Cole and Kyle. "He left for work. Then I saw that he forgot his name tag, so I went running down the street to catch him. I was on my way back to the house when it exploded. What happened?"

Elliot hung his head. "I think the Goblins blew it up."

"Fine time for making jokes." Wendy put her hands on her hips. "Okay, well, let's see if we can get everything cleaned up before Mom and Dad get home from work."

"I didn't make this mess, so I'm not cleaning it up," Cole said.

"I'll clean up my exploded room parts, but that's all," Kyle said.

"I don't think it matters," Elliot said. "Mom and Dad are pretty smart. I think they're going to notice when they sit down for dinner tonight that THE ENTIRE HOUSE IS GONE!"

"Of course they'll notice," Wendy said. "But we've got to have dinner somewhere, and I think it's better to have it in an organized blown-up house than a messy one. That's all I'm saying."

"Well, you'll have to burn our dinner somewhere else tonight," Elliot said. "I'm not hungry anyway."

He stomped off back into the woods. Wendy called after him, but he had bigger problems than his sister's hurt feelings. Mr. Willimaker waited for him at the edge of the trees, right at the border of sunlight and shadow. "What a waste of a perfectly good house," Mr. Willimaker said. "Well, a somewhat good house anyway."

Elliot turned back to the smoky pile of rubble. "When I said I'd become king, I didn't know things would go this far. I'm just a kid. I can't protect myself from the Goblins. Now it looks as if I can't protect my family. I can't save the Brownies either."

"I have to tell you something," Mr. Willimaker muttered

nervously. "Something I should have told you at the very start. The truth is that Queen Bipsy didn't exactly give me your name. She told me to choose the king, and I was the one who wrote in your name, because you saved Patches three Halloweens ago. I never thought the Brownies would let a human become king. I never thought any of this would happen."

"So I'm not really the king?" Elliot asked.

"Not if you don't want to be."

Elliot shrugged. "I'm just not sure if I'm right for the job. But I have to finish what the Goblins started. After that, I'll decide whether I'll stay as king."

"But what are you going to do?" Mr. Willimaker knotted his fingers together. If he twisted his hands any longer, he might never get them apart again.

Elliot pushed his jaw forward. "If I can't go to the Underworld, then I'm bringing the Underworld here. We're going to rescue Patches. Then we'll find out who is helping the Goblins. Then we're going to teach the Goblins a lesson once and for all."

Mr. Willimaker bowed low to Elliot. "At least for now, my friend, I'm very glad that you're our king."

Chapter 20

Where the Family Goes to Jail

ELLIOT'S FATHER WASN'T AS ANGRY AS ELLIOT HAD EXPECTED him to be about their blown-up house. Or maybe he was just in shock.

"The staircase had a squeak in it," he said, staring at where the staircase used to be. "I guess that's not a problem now. But that's all right if we don't have a staircase, since there's no more upstairs. If anyone did try to go up the staircase, they'd just fall off at the top."

On the other hand, Elliot's mother just shook her head and about every ten seconds would mumble, "Oh dear, oh dear." Elliot also noticed she had stopped blinking. That probably wasn't good.

The police had been at the house for three hours trying to figure out why it blew up. Uncle Rufus confessed that maybe his passing gas had somehow blown up the house, but the police said they were sure that wasn't the cause. Passing gas has only been rumored to blow up a house one time in Sprite's Hollow, and that was supposedly after the owner gorged on some very spicy chili for an entire year. Elliot knew that unless the police had Goblins on their list of suspects, they'd never find the real answer.

Wendy shambled by Elliot with a pitcher of water in her hands. Elliot wondered where she'd found it. "You thirsty?" she asked him.

"Nah. Sorry about what I said before, about you burning our food."

Wendy smiled. "Don't worry about it. I'll be burning our food again in no time." Then she hurried over to offer their mother a drink.

"I can't believe it!" Agatha said, walking up behind Elliot. "Why, this is unexpected. I don't remember cursing your house."

Elliot sighed. "It wasn't you, Agatha. The Goblins did this."

"Oh. I hoped I had cursed your house to explode. Then I'd know I had my powers back."

"You've always had them," Elliot said. "You just weren't doing your rhymes correctly."

Agatha tilted her head toward Elliot. "What do you mean?"

"The last words in all your curses. They're not the right words. You say 'sung to by a pea' when you mean 'stung by a bee.' Or 'eat something hairy' when you mean 'meet something scary.'"

Agatha drew back. "I meant something hairy. Like a Yeti."

"Yetis aren't real."

Agatha laughed in a way that made Elliot think maybe she knew something he didn't. A shiver ran down his spine, and he said, "Anyway, the only time you got the rhyme right is when you cursed me to meet the Goblin leader alone. I figure that's still going to happen."

Agatha's voice softened. "Everyone gets cursed at times in their life, Elliot. The trick is, can you look past the cursing? Can you see it for what it is? Take your house, for example. Beyond the exploded pieces, what do you see?"

Elliot shrugged. "I guess I'm really lucky that nobody got blown up inside my house. And it wasn't that great a house anyway, so we haven't lost much." He sat up straight as an idea came to him. "And maybe it'll help me end this war. I know what I have to do!" He turned back to Agatha, and his eyes widened.

She was still Agatha, but her tattered dress was flowing and perfectly white. Her knotted gray hair was gone, replaced by long, silky blonde curls that waved softly in the breeze. Her warty, oatmeal skin was now creamy and soft. He couldn't tell how old she was, because she was ageless. Uncle Rufus was right. She looked like an angel.

"You're beautiful," Elliot whispered.

"I always was," she replied. "You just didn't know it until now."

"I need you to stay with me, please, Agatha. I have to fight the Goblins, and I need your help."

"No, you don't. All you need is the Brownies, and all they need is you. You are their king and you will save them." With that, she clapped her hands together and began to walk away.

"Where are you going?" Elliot asked.

"To say good-bye to your Uncle Rufus. Now that I can curse again, I have places to go."

"Hey, if you happen to see this boy named Tubs Lawless, give him an extra curse for me," he called after her.

Agatha pressed her lips together and then said, "A boy like Tubs doesn't need me to curse him. He has enough problems."

Elliot shook his head. Tubs didn't have problems. He *was* the problem. "Yeah? What problems does he have?"

Agatha turned and her clear, green eyes pierced straight through to Elliot's mind. "His problem is that one day you'll figure out who you are. Then he won't be able to bully you anymore, Your Highness."

Agatha gave Elliot a gentle bow and then walked over and spoke to Rufus. He looked sad for only a moment until she reached up and kissed his cheek. Then his face lit up. He beamed and wished her a warm good-bye.

Reed came to stand beside Elliot as they watched Agatha leave. "I'm glad she's going," Reed whispered. "I know letting her stay with us was the right thing to do, but she was the scariest-looking thing I've ever seen."

"She's not scary," Elliot said. "She's a beautiful young woman. I was lucky to have met her. We all were."

Reed chuckled. "Careful. Whatever's the matter with Uncle Rufus, it looks like you're catching it too."

After Agatha was out of sight, Uncle Rufus ran a hand across his head and then marched over to two policemen and talked with them. A few minutes later, they all walked over to Elliot's parents.

"What did you steal now?" Mother said to Uncle Rufus. "We've got a bigger problem to deal with here."

"No, it's good news this time," Uncle Rufus said. "These

nice officers have arrested me so many times we've become quite good friends. They want to help us with our blown-up house. They said the jail is nearly empty tonight, so if we want to stay there for a day or two, they'll let us stay for free."

Mother shook her head, but Rufus added, "The meals are good, and the beds aren't too bad. The only fellow in the jail right now is another friend of mine. Perfectly harmless."

"What's he in jail for?" Father asked.

"He steals the wool off sheep. Sneaks into their pen and shears them in the middle of the night. So as long as we don't bring any sheep into the jail, we'll be fine."

Father shrugged. Mother sighed. Then Rufus smiled and clapped his hands together. "Okay! The Penster family is going to jail!"

"Yay!" Cole and Kyle gave each other high fives.

"Er, I'm going to stay with friends tonight," Elliot said. His friends were the Brownies, but he didn't think his parents needed that detail.

Mother folded her arms the way all moms do when they're not sure something is a good idea. "Do I know these friends?"

"They've been to our house a lot lately," Elliot said, quite truthfully.

Father brushed a hand over Elliot's hair the way dads do when they're trying to get Mom's permission. "Just tell your friends that your family is in jail and to call if there are any problems."

Mother smiled. "Elliot's just an eleven-year-old kid, dear. I don't think he'll have any problems tonight."

Elliot didn't think so either. Not unless the Goblins succeeded in destroying all the Brownies and also got rid of him. That would definitely be considered a problem.

Father said, "Okay, but it sounds as if you'll miss out on quite an adventure with us."

"Don't worry," Elliot said. "I'm sure I'll have an adventure of my own." As soon as his family left, Elliot sat down with Mr. Willimaker in the woods. "How many Brownies can come here?"

Mr. Willimaker sighed. "I can't get them to come. What Fudd told you before was true. I am a joke in Burrowsville. The last time I tried to warn everyone of danger, it turned out to be nothing but a little mouse. They won't listen to me this time."

Elliot leaned in to Mr. Willimaker. "You *have* to make them listen. Maybe you were a joke before, but now you have a message straight from the king. I know you can do this."

Mr. Willimaker smiled. "You're right. I can do it. I will do it." He began counting on his fingers. "A few will need to stay behind and look after the young ones. I suppose we might close the shops early and that will spare some more." He looked up at Elliot. "Would a couple hundred Brownies be enough?"

Elliot smiled. "Yes, but I need them right away. We have a lot to do before dark. Tell everyone to wear work clothes."

Mr. Willimaker straightened his back, making him at least a half-inch taller, which is a lot for a Brownie. He stuck out his chest and said, "Work clothes are a Brownies' only clothes. Even if I lose my voice, I won't stop talking until they agree to come."

"I also need to meet with my royal advisors," Elliot said, then added, "Do I have any royal advisors?"

"Just Fudd Fartwick, I suppose," Mr. Willimaker said. "He was Queen Bipsy's closest advisor."

"I want to speak with him, then," Elliot said. "And you as well. You have been my closest advisor."

Mr. Willimaker bowed very low and then poofed himself gone. While he waited, Elliot sat down on the ground to think about his plan. He hadn't done so much thinking since learning double-digit multiplication. This thinking was so much work that Elliot didn't hear the footsteps creep up behind him.

A hand grabbed Elliot's shoulder. He heard Tubs Lawless snarling at him in his usual mean voice, "Okay, Penster, now you're gonna get what's coming to you!"

Chapter 21

Where Elliot Shares His Lemon Pie

WHEN TUBS LAWLESS TELLS A KID HE'S GOING TO GET what's coming to him, that's usually a sign that the kid will need several bandages. But Elliot's bandages were somewhere in the blown-up house, so all he could do was turn around slowly and hope he didn't end up wishing *he* had been in the blown-up house.

Tubs stretched out his hands toward Elliot, but in them was something Elliot hadn't expected. A lemon pie.

"My mom said that we have to bring this to you, since your house blew up," Tubs said. "I hope you're happy. This was supposed to be my dessert tonight."

"Er, thanks." Elliot kept waiting for Tubs to do whatever he'd really come to do, like push the pie in Elliot's face and laugh, or run away when Elliot reached for it.

"Do you want the pie or not?" Tubs asked.

Elliot shrugged and took it. "Smells good."

"I wouldn't know. I haven't been able to smell anything since I was five years old and shoved a bunch of chocolate candies up my nose."

Maybe the candies had worked their way up to Tubs's brain. It would explain a lot. But Elliot only said, "Well, tell your mom thanks."

Tubs began walking away but then turned back and said, "You know, since you just took my family's dessert, I should probably take something from you too."

Elliot waved his hand toward the pile of his blown-up house. "Take whatever you want." It didn't matter to him.

Tubs kicked around a few wooden boards and then pointed to a trunk. It wasn't just any trunk. This one had been in Elliot's room until the other night when it started making noises again. Elliot had dragged it into the hallway so he could sleep. The trunk was dented from the explosion and one of the handles had come off, but it was still in one piece. "I'm going to take that."

It had been making noise because it still had three Goblins in it. "Not that trunk," Elliot said, jumping up. "I meant you could take anything else."

Tubs held up a fist. Elliot had seen that fist up close plenty of times and stopped in place.

"Don't tell me what I can or can't take of yours," Tubs said. "Enjoy my mom's pie—or else!" With that, he picked up the trunk and dragged it behind him, huffing and puffing.

Elliot started to go after him but was stopped by Mr. Willimaker returning with Fudd Fartwick.

"Will the Goblins hurt Tubs?" Elliot asked.

Mr. Willimaker stared after Tubs. "Hard to say. They'll either be so happy to get out of the trunk that they'll barely hurt him at all. Or they'll be so mad about having been locked in the trunk that they'll chew his arms off." Mr. Willimaker shrugged. "He'll probably be fine."

"I hope so," Elliot said. "Or else everyone will call him Tubs Armless instead. Ha! Now tell me about the Brownies. Did you talk to them?"

Mr. Willimaker nodded. It hadn't gone well at first. It had started with him poofing to the center of Burrowsville and announcing that the Brownies were in danger. The Brownies only laughed at him and asked if it was another field mouse invasion.

Then Mr. Willimaker did something so extreme, so out of his usual character that all the Brownies had to listen: he loosened his bow tie.

He loosened his bow tie to make it easier to jump up and down, which messed up his neatly combed hair. Then he yelled, "Burrowsville needs you! Your king needs you! You will listen to me because for once in our lives the Brownies are going to fight back!"

Now, as he faced Elliot, Mr. Willimaker couldn't help but smile with pride. He bowed low and said, "I did it, Your Highness. The Brownies are coming."

"I knew you could do it." Elliot turned to Fudd. "I'm glad you're here too."

Fudd looked at Elliot, then at the house. Then back at Elliot. Of course, Fudd had known that the Goblins were going to blow up Elliot's house. He didn't realize Elliot would survive the explosion, though.

Fudd's eyes got so wide they almost popped out of his head. "This is crazy! Couldn't they even blow up your house correctly?"

"What?" Elliot and Mr. Willimaker both asked.

Fudd paused and then said, "I meant, the Goblins must've been crazy to blow up your house. I assume you have a plan for revenge. Perhaps to throw that lemon pie you're holding at them."

Elliot set the pie down and shook his head. "Revenge never makes things better. I just want to stop this war." He turned to Mr. Willimaker. "Get all the Brownies to dig a big circle in the clearing in the forest. Leave an island in the center." Mr. Willimaker bowed and scampered off.

"What's the island for?" Fudd asked.

"I'm going to lure all the Goblins to that island." Elliot pointed to a clump of trees at the edge of the woods. "I'll hide alone beside those trees. When the Goblins arrive, I'll trap them."

Fudd nodded. "Very clever. What do you need me to do?"

"I need you to go to the Goblins. Tell them they can surrender now and stop this war against me and the Brownies. If they don't, then I'll stop them myself."

A sly smile crossed Fudd's face. "You'll stop them? Waiting all alone beside those trees?"

"That's right."

"Really? Just sitting there? Like you've got nothing better to do than wait for a bunch of angry Goblins?"

Elliot shrugged. "I don't have anything better to do." He really didn't.

Fudd gave his most evil laugh. He had put a lot of practice into his laugh, so for an evil Brownie, it was very impressive.

"What was that?" Elliot asked.

Fudd coughed. "Er, I meant to laugh like this." Then he gave a little giggle. "What about that one?"

"Your other laugh was better. Use that one with the Goblins and they're sure to give up." Elliot picked up the lemon pie. "By the way, do you want to have this?"

"Your pie?"

"Sure. It's not payment for helping me, because I know

Brownies don't like that. So it's a gift. Not from a king to an advisor. Just friend to friend."

Fudd took the pie and sniffed it deeply. "Are you sure? This whole pie for me?"

"It's all yours," Elliot said. "Lemons give me the sniffles anyway."

A tear welled up in Fudd's eye. He thought way back to his childhood, to the girl who had laughed when he had asked for a turn on the swing, even after he said "please." He'd never had a real friend since that day. Now there was someone who did want to be Fudd's friend, and of all the bad luck, it just happened to be someone Fudd was trying to kill. "Look at that. Your pie is giving me the sniffles too." He pushed it toward Elliot. "I can't accept this. You should give it to Mr. Willimaker. He's been a much better friend to you than I have."

"But you're one of the Brownies, which makes you my friend too." Elliot looked back to the woods, then said to Fudd, "You'd better hurry to go talk to the Goblins. I'm almost ready for them here."

"Thank you, King Elliot. I want you to know that if the Goblins ever do succeed in killing you, I'll always feel a little bad about that." With his arms around the pie, Fudd bowed and poofed himself away.

"What else do you need?" Mr. Willimaker said, running up to Elliot. "The circle digging has begun."

Elliot explained the rest of his plan to Mr. Willimaker and then put a hand on his shoulder and said, "I haven't forgotten about Patches. We'll get her back, okay?"

Mr. Willimaker bowed gratefully. "I trust you, King Elliot. But how will you get the Goblins to come here?"

Elliot pointed to Reed's very large jar of pickle relish. "Didn't you tell me that Goblins love pickles?"

"Oh, yes."

"What about pickle relish? I bet they love it too."

Mr. Willimaker grinned. The jar was as tall as he was, a little bit wider, and far more see-through. Somewhere in Flog were hundreds of Goblins who had, in their wildest and craziest dreams, hoped to find a treasure like this one day. Every Goblin in Flog would come to eat as much as they could. They loved pickles more than anything else, and now pickles were going to be their downfall.

Chapter 22

Where Fudd Gets Burned

WHAT'S THAT AROUND YOUR MOUTH?" GRISSEL ASKED Fudd. "It's yellow."

"Lemon pie." Fudd smeared his mouth across his sleeve. He'd stopped before entering Flog to eat the lemon pie King Elliot had given him. He thought he'd feel less guilty about working with the Goblins if he couldn't see the pie anymore, but for some reason, eating it had only made things worse. His stomach growled at him in a rather accusing way. Fudd tapped his foot on the ground and silently ordered his stomach to be quiet. He had bigger worries than an upset tummy.

"So let me make sure I understand," Grissel said. "You're telling me that King Elliot is just going to wait, all by himself, in some trees to catch us Goblins? Doesn't he know how much stronger we are than he is?"

Fudd threw up his hands. "He thinks he can get all of you into his forest and trap you there." He noticed a little lemon pudding on one of his fingers and licked it. Every lick sent a shock of guilt through him. Sweet, delicious guilt.

Grissel knocked Fudd's hands away. "How will he trap us?"

"It doesn't matter, because it won't work," Fudd said. "You and I will poof directly there and capture him, and then you're free to get rid of him."

Grissel smiled. "You said Elliot has the Brownies in those woods?"

"Yes."

"Then I'll bring all my Goblins. Once we've captured Elliot, I'll make sure that my Goblins finally destroy the Brownies!"

Fudd rubbed his hands together nervously. That had not been part of his plan. "But we agreed that I'd become king of the Brownies."

"You can become king of anyone we don't eat."

"And what about Patches?" Fudd cringed as he asked the question, worried about the answer.

A wicked glint crossed Grissel's eyes. "She's fine. For now. But that will probably change tonight."

Panic welled inside Fudd, choking him. "No, Grissel. No, you can't."

"Who's going to stop me? You?" Grissel bared his sharp teeth and let out a low growl. "I'll do whatever I want. Now come with me."

At this point, Fudd had no choice but to follow Grissel, but when they left Grissel's home, he saw Goblins already poofing themselves away. Some of them licked their lips. Some rubbed their hands together in excitement.

Grissel grabbed one of them. "Where's everyone going?"

"Can't you smell the pickles? Hurry before they're all gone!" With that, the Goblin poofed himself away.

Grissel sniffed the air. The sour smell of vinegar and cucumbers filled his nose. It came from the human world. A line of drool ran down Grissel's chin, and he grinned hungrily at Fudd.

"Remember the pickles," Fudd said, waving his hands and taking two steps back. "Goblins should eat more pickles and fewer Brownies."

Grissel watched as the last of his pickle-hungry Goblins poofed themselves to King Elliot's woods.

"It's a good thing I already decided to let them go," Grissel said. "Because otherwise they'd be in a lot of trouble for leaving without me."

Fudd sadly shook his head. He hoped the Goblins would find the pickles before they found any Brownies. He couldn't help but feel a little responsible for what was happening.

Grissel grabbed Fudd by the arm. "Now you and I will teach the human king it's not wise to trick Goblins."

Grissel poofed himself and Fudd to a spot just outside the trees. From there they could see a large pile of pickle relish. Every Goblin from Flog was gathered around the pile, fighting for as many bites as they could get. Several of them were so busy clawing at each other that no Goblin could get any relish.

"They're not trapped here at all," Grissel said happily. "Your king doesn't know as much about Goblins as I thought."

"Maybe they'll fill up on the pickle relish," Fudd whispered. "They won't be hungry for Brownies."

"We're always hungry for Brownies," Grissel said, licking his lips with his crooked blue tongue.

Fudd didn't like the sound of that, but he continued walking toward Elliot's hiding place in the trees. Grissel followed closely behind him. Too close. Fudd walked faster. He thought he heard Grissel smelling him.

When they arrived in the woods, they found Elliot facing them, relaxing with his back against a large oak tree. He didn't seem surprised to see them. He didn't look afraid either, which worried Fudd. This was the point in the plan when Elliot should have begun to look terrified.

"You were the only one who knew where I'd be hiding," Elliot said to Fudd. "And now you've brought the Goblin leader here to me."

Fudd still tasted the lemon pie in his mouth, which was a little sourer now than he remembered. It had been a gift from Elliot, and he repaid that gift by bringing Grissel here. Rule number four in the *Guidebook to Evil Plans* clearly stated, "Never accept a gift of kindness from your mortal enemy" (page 12). Fudd had never really understood the meaning of that rule…until now. He kicked a foot in the dirt, ashamed of himself.

"You've been helping the Goblins try to get me," Elliot added. "Why?"

Fudd's lower lip quivered. Ever since he learned that Grissel would be eating his friends, he'd begun to think working with him wasn't such a good idea. "This is all my fault. More than anything I wanted to be king, but I know now I was wrong. I'm so sorry."

"Well, I'm not sorry," Grissel snarled, pushing his way past Fudd. "I still want to get rid of you, human. I already scared you half to death. It's time to finish the job."

Elliot smiled. "Better get close enough that I can see you this time."

Grissel growled and took a step toward Elliot. Grissel's foot landed on a rope that instantly went tight around his bony foot and pulled him up into the air. In a panic, Fudd stepped to the side and into another rope that yanked him up beside Grissel. They dangled upside down, their bodies swinging softly in midair. Fudd clasped his hands together and waited until his body turned to face Elliot, then said, "Forgive me, Your Highness."

Elliot marched right up to Grissel and Fudd and said, "These are my dad's traps. I've been in them myself, so I know you can't get yourself free. If you're both very good, I'll let you out before my dad finds out and tries to have you for dinner. I order you both not to poof out of there. I order all Goblins not to poof away from here."

"You think you can defeat me that easily?" Grissel said with a sneer. "Release me now or else."

"Or else what?" Elliot asked.

Grissel pointed high up to a tree that stood over the pile of Goblins and the pickle relish. Two more Goblins had appeared there. Tied up in a rope dangling from their hands was Patches. If they let go of the rope, she would fall right onto the backs of the Goblins.

Grissel showed his jagged teeth as he laughed. "You've lost, little king. Release me now, or else they get your favorite Brownie for dessert!"

Chapter 23

Where Elliot Gets Some Fresh Air

ELLIOT RAN TO WHERE HE COULD GET A BETTER LOOK AT Patches. The Goblins had tied the rope several times around her whole body. She wouldn't be able to wiggle free on her own, and even if she did, there was nowhere she could go but down onto the pile of Goblins. Several had already smelled her and left the pickle pile to stand beneath her with their arms out. When her rope dropped, they wanted to be the first to get her.

"Help!" Patches cried. "Elliot, help me!"

"You have ten seconds before I order them to drop her," Grissel hissed. "Eighteen!"

Elliot turned. "I have eighteen seconds?"

Grissel rolled his eyes. "Didn't you hear me? Ten seconds. I didn't say which ten. Now it's seventeen!"

Mr. Willimaker ran to Elliot's side and tugged on his

shirt. "That's my daughter. Please, Your Highness, we have to save her."

"Can't she just poof away?" Elliot asked.

"She's Grissel's prisoner. If he ordered her not to poof away, then she can't. Just like Grissel can't poof away from here until you allow it."

"Sixteen!" Grissel said.

"Let me go up there," Mr. Willimaker said, beginning to flap his hands nervously.

"You're not strong enough to stop them." Elliot took a deep breath. He didn't want to admit that he was sort of scared to say the next part, but there was no choice. "Poof me up there."

The Goblins holding Patches began playing with the rope. They swung her in a little circle so that the Goblins below would have to run to catch her when she fell.

"Stop that!" Patches yelled, wiggling angrily. "I'm not a swing!"

"Fifteen!" Grissel said.

"Poof me up there," Elliot repeated. His heart pounded and his fingers felt numb, but he had made his decision.

Mr. Willimaker shook his head. "I told you before, Brownies don't have enough magic to poof humans. I'd send part of you up there, but the rest of you might not make it."

"Thirteen!" Grissel said.

"You're on number fourteen!" Elliot said.

"Never heard of that number," Grissel yelled back. "Twelve!"

"Poof me now," Elliot said to Mr. Willimaker. "Do it, or else they're going to drop her."

"Even for a Brownie, my magic isn't powerful enough," Mr. Willimaker protested, wringing his hands together. "Maybe a stronger Brownie could do it, but not me."

From behind them, they heard a small and much humbler voice than usual. "I could try," Fudd said.

"What?" Grissel snarled. "Whose side are you on?"

"I'll never be on your side again," Fudd said. "That was my terrible, unforgivable mistake." As his rope swung him again to face Elliot, he added, "Your Highness, I know there's no reason you should trust me. But Mr. Willimaker will tell you that I'm the only Brownie strong enough to attempt poofing you. I don't know if I can do it, but I do know there's no other Brownie strong enough to try."

"Just for that, I'm skipping to ten." Grissel stuck his long, snakelike tongue out at Fudd. "Ha! That'll show you."

Mr. Willimaker tugged on Elliot's shirt again. "Fudd is stronger than me, sir. But this is still too dangerous. Even though she's my daughter, I can't risk the life of our king."

"Nine!" Grissel said. "Release me now, or it'll be too late for Patches."

Elliot closed his eyes, took another deep breath, and then calmly turned to Fudd. "Poof me up there now, Fudd. I know you can do it."

"I'll do my best, King Elliot." Fudd closed his eyes and snapped his fat fingers together.

Dear Reader, generally speaking, poofing is not a bad way to travel. It's quick, painless, and at worst, only a little bit ticklish. But it's always best to be prepared, or else poofing tends to confuse the brain for a moment as it tries to figure out how to keep all the body parts together during the trip.

Since humans aren't used to getting poofed around, they should always start with a creature that has a lot of experience. The Brownies have no experience in poofing other creatures to places. None. Zip. Zero. It would have been better for Fudd to practice this trick a few hundred times with tiny worms who wouldn't mind if they arrived somewhere without their arms or legs, because they have no arms or legs.

However, Fudd had no time to practice. And no second chances. In less than a second, Grissel would order his Goblins to drop Patches. Elliot was the only one who could save her.

To Elliot, getting poofed somewhere by a Brownie felt as if a bunch of invisible hands had grabbed every part of his body and pulled them all in whatever order they wanted to the top of the tree. It didn't exactly hurt, but it wasn't comfortable either. When he opened his eyes (after his eyes were returned to their sockets), he was standing beside two surprised Goblins on a tree branch high above the pile of Goblins below.

One of the Goblins lunged at Elliot, claws out. Elliot ducked and the Goblin flew directly over his head. He flapped his arms as he began to fall. Not being a bird, he continued falling, landing on some Goblins below who had been hoping to catch the far more edible Patches.

Elliot stood again, trying to regain his balance. Then he noticed one very important detail. His left arm was gone. Fudd had gotten most of him here, but not all. He fell onto the thick tree branch and with his right hand grabbed a bunch of leaves to keep from falling. He locked his legs around the branch and steadied himself.

"Where's my arm, Fudd?" he yelled.

"I'm working on it, Your Highness!" Fudd called back.

"Eight!" Grissel screamed from his upside-down trap. "Eight, you idiot. Eight!"

The Goblin holding Patches looked confused for a moment, as if he couldn't figure out the importance of the number eight. Then Grissel yelled, "Drop her!"

"I thought that was on seven," the Goblin called back.

"Do it now!" Grissel yelled again.

The next few seconds passed so fast, Elliot would never

be sure exactly how it all happened. He let go of the leaves that were keeping him steady and, while tightening his legs around the branch, swung his weight downward. The Goblin holding Patches released her rope, which fluttered in the air past him. He tried to grab it once, but it slipped through his hand. He tried again, and this time he somehow kept a hold on it, although Patches was so close to the Goblins now they could almost reach her if they jumped high enough.

The weight of catching Patches caused the branch to bow, and then it sprang back up like a rubber band. The Goblin who had been holding Patches hadn't considered the importance of holding on to anything other than the rope, and as the branch rebounded he flew into the air and then fell back to the earth like a Goblin-shaped rocket. He landed on another two Goblins who were trying to jump up and reach Patches.

Still upside down with his legs locked around the branch of the tree, Elliot felt Patches's rope begin to slip. With only one arm, he knew he couldn't hold on to her much longer. But he had no way to pull her up.

"You're not Grissel's prisoner anymore," Mr. Willimaker shouted to Patches. "Elliot has you. Now poof out of there!"

Patches closed her eyes, and Elliot felt the weight of the rope disappear. He looked over to Mr. Willimaker and saw her poof close to her father, who grabbed her in a tight hug.

"Where's my arm?" Elliot called to Fudd. If he fell, he wouldn't last long against the Goblins below.

"Wish me luck." Fudd snapped his fingers, and Elliot's arm returned to his body. But something was still wrong.

"I don't need two arms on my right side!" Elliot said as his left arm appeared just below his right arm. "Fix this!"

"Sorry about that," Fudd said.

With another snap, the arm reappeared where it should be, properly attached to the left side of his body. Elliot wiggled it a few times to make sure it was going to stay in place, then used his arms to pull himself back onto the branch.

"We can poof you down now," Mr. Willimaker said.

"No, thanks." Elliot didn't want to get poofed anywhere ever again. He pulled the rope up with him and tied it around the branch. Holding tightly to the knots on the other end, where Patches had been, he took a running leap into the air.

Okay, so it didn't swing him back to the ground quite as well as he had pictured it. But in a clumsy sort of way, it did get him away from the Goblins where he fell onto the ground not far from Mr. Willimaker. It would have been nice if he could have landed on his feet, because landing on his hands and face didn't seem very king-like. But at least he landed with all of his body parts in one piece and where they should be. Plus, Patches was safe.

She ran to him with a hug that nearly choked him. "Thank you, thank you, thank you!"

"Welcome back," Elliot said, getting to his feet. "But this isn't over yet."

"You're right about that," Grissel said. "Because my Goblins are just about finished eating that pickle relish. And if they can't poof away, then they'll have nothing better to do than attack you."

"I don't think so." Elliot pulled his crown off his wrist and placed it on his head. It was a little small, but still a crown. It was time to end the war.

Where There's an Island in the Woods

Elliot had put the pickle relish in a very special place in the woods, on an island. Of course, it didn't look like an island at all. Instead, it looked like pieces of Elliot's exploded home had fallen into the woods and landed in a wide circle around a pile of pickle relish. What the Goblins didn't know was that the Brownies had put the pieces of wood from Elliot's home around the island where the Goblins were able to cross over them like bridges. They were so excited to get to the pickle relish, they never thought about what was beneath that wood.

It was time for them to think about it.

Elliot stepped out from the trees and yelled to the Brownies, "Remove the wood!"

Brownies appeared from their hiding places. There were more of them than the Goblins could count (which isn't saying much, since few Goblins besides Grissel can count higher than eight, their number of fingers). There were boys and girls, young and old, and all of them stood ready to obey their human king.

Each Brownie grabbed a single board and dragged it away from the island. It left the Goblins surrounded by at least a foot of water. The hose that Cole and Kyle played with every day was flooding the trench. A few Goblins tested the water with a toe or finger then pulled it out with a water welt on their green skin.

The Goblins hissed and scowled and shouted insults at the Brownies: "Your mother makes chocolate cake!" and "Pickles and Brownies taste good together!"

Elliot ran up to the island and stood on a large rock so that all the Goblins could see him. "Listen to me," he yelled. "It's time for the war between the Goblins and Brownies to end!"

The Goblins booed, the Brownies cheered, and a little squirrel who had wandered onto the tree branch overhead quickly scampered away. (As nearly everyone knows, squirrels have never been interested in interspecies wars.) Elliot held up a hand for them to be quiet and then proclaimed, "This war has been going on for a long time. You're so used to all this trouble that it seems normal to you. But from now on, friendship will be normal. Peace will be normal. I know Goblins are used to eating Brownies, but now you must learn to only eat things that want to be eaten. Brownies, I know you're used to losing in this war, but it's time to stop thinking of yourself as losers. You're too great to think that way. It's not who we are anymore."

Elliot paused and thought of Tubs. Tubs...who chased Elliot across town, and made Elliot do his homework, and who almost flushed Elliot down the toilet. Agatha had said Tubs's problem was that one day Elliot would figure out who he was. Elliot smiled. It was so wide that his smile almost stretched off his face. Maybe what Agatha had said would happen one day just had happened.

Elliot decided he wasn't going to accept bullying from Tubs anymore either. Just as he was helping the Brownies stand up for themselves, he planned to stand up for himself from now on too. He stood even taller on his rock, like a true king would.

"Here's the deal. Any Goblin who promises to live in peace with the Brownies will get to come off the island. If you make this promise, you can return to Flog. We'll become friends and learn to help each other. If you won't promise to live in peace, then you will have to learn to live on this island."

Elliot watched as several of the Goblins tried to poof themselves off. But he'd already commanded them not to leave, and they were too afraid of the water to cross the island. They truly were trapped.

After a number of failed tries at leaving on his own, a tall Goblin with an extra-long nose stepped forward and raised his hand. "King Elliot? I will promise."

Elliot walked forward so that he stood across the water from the Goblin. "You won't eat any more Brownies?"

The Goblin raised his hand. "May I be forced to eat choco-late cake all the rest of my life if I eat another Brownie."

"Then be a friend to us, and we'll be a friend to you." Elliot nodded his head at several Brownies near him, who lowered their boards and helped the Goblin cross off the island. "You can poof home," Elliot told him.

With a short, respectful bow to Elliot, the Goblin snapped his fingers and left.

175

In turn, nearly every other Goblin did the same. Some went home right away, some stayed to talk with other Brownies, setting up pickle trades and sharing ideas on Underworld gardening.

Suddenly very tired, Elliot leaned against a tree, watching the Goblins and Brownies as they worked together. Beside him, he felt a tug on his shirt.

"Your Highness, I couldn't wait any longer to thank you," Mr. Willimaker said, holding Patches by the hand. She danced from one foot to the other, clearly excited to be back with her father. Patches scampered over to Elliot, bowed before him, and then leapt into his arms and gave him a hug.

"You saved me from the Goblins," Patches said, punching Elliot lightly on the arm. "That was really cool."

"I think you saved me from the Goblins too," Elliot said. "We're even."

Patches blushed. "I might have helped a little bit." She told Elliot about escaping from the hole and then hiding in the carrot cave where she was captured again.

Elliot didn't know what a carrot cave was. Maybe he'd ask about that later.

"I was pretty mad when they caught me again," Patches said. "I really enjoyed those carrots. Dad says I ate so many I'm going to turn orange for a week!" Patches rubbed her belly with a hand that Elliot thought already looked a little orange, and then she let out a giant-size burp. Nobody who is only two feet tall has ever let out a burp such as this one. Earthquake scientists hundreds of miles away rushed to their monitors to see what happened. Astronauts orbiting the earth saw the entire planet shake just a little. And Mr. Willimaker laughed. He had missed Patches very much.

"We shouldn't ever have trouble with the Goblins again," Elliot said. "The Goblin war is over."

In the end, every single Goblin left the island in the woods. The Brownies cheered again when the last one left. They hugged each other and then bowed together before Elliot.

Elliot raised his hands again for them to be silent. He took the crown off his head and gave it to Mr. Willimaker, then said, "There's something you all should know. Queen Bipsy never gave Mr. Willimaker my name to be king. She told him to choose a name, and he chose mine. If you all want to have someone else as king, a Brownie maybe, I'll understand."

There was silence as the Brownies looked at each other. Then Patches said, "Your Highness, everything is as it should be. My father did exactly what Queen Bipsy told him to do. When he wrote your name, he was following her command."

"That's right," Mr. Willimaker said. "When I chose you, I did obey her."

Patches continued, "We know you're the king, because when you commanded the Goblins not to poof away, they had to obey you. They would only have to obey a real king."

"Hail King Elliot," the Brownies cheered. "Long live King Elliot!"

Mr. Willimaker pushed the crown back into Elliot's hands. "Your Highness, the Brownies need you. Patches was right. You are our king."

Elliot smiled and put the crown back on his head. "Then as your king, I will finish this." He marched over to the ropes where Grissel and Fudd were still hanging. Their upside-down faces had turned slightly purple, but otherwise they were fine.

"Your war is finished," Elliot told Grissel. "There are no more Goblins who'll fight with you."

"I saw them leave, the cowards." Grissel folded his arms. "Fine, I'll make the promise too. Now let me go home."

"He's crossing his fingers," Fudd said. "I can see him from here. Don't believe his promise, Your Highness."

Elliot shook his head at Grissel, disappointed to see he'd try something as sneaky as crossed fingers. "Mr. Willimaker, take Grissel to the Brownie prison. I want him to receive the most chocolaty chocolate cake we have, every single day, without frosting or milk, until he truly agrees to become a friend to the Brownies."

Mr. Willimaker nodded, and then both he and Grissel disappeared.

Elliot turned to Fudd, who wiped a tear from his eye.

"I suppose you'll want me to have chocolate cake now too," Fudd whimpered.

"You helped me save Patches," Elliot said. "If you still wanted me dead, that would've been your chance."

"I've changed," Fudd said. "I hope I can show you that."

"It will take me a long time to trust you again," Elliot said. "If anyone tries to get me, you have to understand that I might wonder if you're involved."

Fudd scrunched up his face. "What do you mean?"

"Let's just say that no one ever blew up my house until I met you." Elliot frowned as he said it, but Fudd thought he might have seen a slight grin as Elliot looked his way.

"It will take me a long time to prove that I can be trusted," Fudd said meekly. "But if you give me the chance, I'll be a much better advisor than before. I'll be a much better Brownie than before. Tell me what I can do to fix things."

Elliot pointed to the mess of his exploded home. "To start, you can get the Brownies to build me another home. I don't need it fancy or new. I don't care if the stairs still squeak. I just want a place for my family to come back to."

For the first time since Elliot had become king, Fudd Fartwick gave him a real bow (which is not easy when one is hanging upside down with a rope around his leg). "Your Highness, it may not be fancy or new, and the stairs might still squeak, but you are a king and the Brownies will build you a castle."

"Then I release you," Elliot said. "You may poof out of that trap."

Fudd snapped his fingers and landed upright on the ground. He bowed to Elliot again and then quickly ducked into the trees as someone behind them yelled, "Penster!"

Elliot turned and saw Tubs Lawless running across his lawn, dragging the trunk he'd taken behind him. Tubs dropped the trunk in the middle of the yard and said, "Penster, it's a good thing your house blew up!"

"Why?" Elliot asked.

"It was probably full of those big green rats I found in this trunk."

"Did they get out?"

"They're back in the trunk now. Finally." Tubs shook a fist at Elliot. "But watch out. I'll get you for letting me steal those things."

"No," Elliot said firmly. "You won't."

Tubs's lip curled in anger. "What did you say?"

"You won't chase me through town. And you won't throw rocks or toys or even your bicycle at me. I'm not going to do your homework for you or let you flush me down the toilet. You are done being a bully."

"Who's gonna make me stop?"

"Me. And those big green rats will help me if I need them. They're my friends now."

Tubs stumbled back a few steps. "Fine. Just keep that trunk away from me!" He turned and ran, revealing long claw marks down the back of his pants.

Elliot smiled as he watched Tubs scramble away. Then, with a happy sigh, he grabbed a hose and walked toward the trunk. A king's work was never done.

The Underworld Chronicles continue...

Elliot and the Pixie Plot

Even though Elliot won the Goblin War for the Brownies, his life isn't exactly painless now. Tubs Lawless isn't bullying Elliot much these days, but now Elliot's got new enemies to deal with. When Elliot finds himself in the middle of a battle between the Pixies and the Fairies, he's going to need the help of his new Brownie friends to survive. Being King of the Brownies isn't always as easy as chocolate and pickles.

Acknowledgments

Thanks always to Jeff, my best friend and true companion. To Ron Peters and Tom Horner, talented authors and friends, for keeping their critiquing axes sharp and honest. Thanks to Ammi-Joan Paquette and Dan Ehrenhaft, for catching the vision of Elliot.

And a final thanks to turnip farmers around the world. Some may say that "hero" is too strong a word for you, but I don't think so. Neither do the Brownies.

About the Author

JENNIFER A. NIELSEN lives at the base of a very tall mountain in Northern Utah with her husband, three children, and a fat lizard. She loves the smell of rainy days, hot chocolate, and old books, preferably all at once. Although she has never actually met any Underworld creatures, she did see someone once who might have been a Troll. Learn more at her website: www.jennielsen.com.

About the Illustrator

GIDEON KENDALL graduated from the Cooper Union for Science and Art with a BFA and has since been working as an artist, illustrator, animation designer, and musician in Brooklyn.

DATE DU